Amish Unrequited

Deidra Scott

Published by Trellis Publishing, 2021.

AMISH UNREQUITED

First edition. July 2, 2021.

ISBN: 979-8224089611

Written by Deidra Scott.

AMISH UNREQUITED

DEIDRA SCOTT

Chapter One

The bright summer sun shone down on Marcus Christner's head full of dark hair as he pulled off his straw hat long enough to wipe some sweat from his forehead. *Summer*. Of all the seasons, summer was his favorite. There was no joy quite like that of watching baby calves dance in the fields around their mothers, the smell of fresh cut hay waiting to be bailed in the fields and apple pies baking in the house, or the sound of frogs croaking on the creek banks at night.

Closing his eyes, Marcus took in a deep breath of warm air before placing his hat back on his head.

Grabbing the reigns to the horses, he urged them along, hurrying them so that he could get some plowing done before the hot day drifted into the night.

"Marcus," the voice of his sister, Annie, made Marcus rein the horses in before they could get a good start on the job ahead, "Marcus!"

Looking across the field, Marcus could see his teenage sister hurrying through the clods of freshly-plowed soil, a glass of lemonade clasped in her hands.

"Here," she handed it to him, a good-natured smile on her pretty face, "I thought you might be getting thirsty."

"*Danke*!" Marcus thanked her as he took the glass in his hands and downed the drink, glad to have the chilly treat.

"You should be glad to have such a fine sister!" Annie announced.

"And you're lucky to have such a good brother." Marcus returned reaching out to give her a playful shove.

"And maybe my kind, wonderful brother would consider giving me a ride to the Amish store before it closes?" Annie suggested with a grin, her true motive finally showing through.

Marcus had to laugh, "Ah, so the drink was just a bribe?"

"Sure was!"

Looking at the work he had left ahead of him, Marcus took a deep breath and let it out slowly, "I suppose this field can wait until morning. *Jah* – sure, just given me about ten minutes to get the horse unhitched."

Annie grinned broadly as she took the empty glass from her brother, "I'll run on in and get ready!"

Sighing deeply, Marcus led the horse across the field and toward his father's barn.

At twenty-two-years-old, Marcus had to admit that he was doing well for himself. He had a good eye for business and, after spending his teenage years working on a construction crew, had saved back enough money to purchase several acres of land that joined his *daed's* farm. Marcus had carefully considered which crops were going to require the least amount of investment while gaining the best profit and had planted them on his land.

Now, four years late, Marcus owned fifty acres of his own land where he grew a large supply of crops. Although he still paid his father to use his horses and equipment, Marcus had enough money in the bank to buy his own if it ever became necessary.

As he unhitched the horse and led him to his stall, Marcus had to recognize that he was achieving success in almost every way possible. There was only one area where he was lacking.

"Are ya ready to go?" The voice of Annie made him jump as he led a fresh horse out of its stall and hitched him to the buggy.

"Climb on up," Marcus instructed her as he snapped the bridle in place.

Sitting down on the buggy seat beside his sister, he tried to push his troubling thoughts out of his mind. Try as he might, Marcus couldn't ignore the fact that, while all the other young men in the community were quickly pairing off and getting engaged, he had never so much as even had a girlfriend. His only consolation was that his older brother, Amos, was still single as well. Perhaps the Christner boys were just destined to become old bachelors.

Almost as if she could read his thoughts, Annie announced, "I guess I might as well tell ya that I won't be needing a ride home from the singing Sunday night."

Marcus raised an eyebrow in surprise, "Did ya decide not to go after all?"

"No, silly!" Annie reached out and gave him a slap on the arm, "I got asked to go home with Jacob Hostetler!" Leaning back against the hard-wood seat she smiled and breathed out slowly, "Jacob Hostetler! Now, there's a fine young man!"

Remaining silent for a moment, Annie finally glanced at her older brother and said, "Ya know, you ought to find you a girl to bring home from the singing."

Marcus felt a lump rising in his throat as he shook his head, "No, I don't think so."

Shaking her head, Annie laughed, "*Ach*, I'm starting to think that you just want to stay single for ever!" Thinking to herself for a moment, she finally announced, "You could just pop in and ask Lucy Schrock when we get to the store."

It felt like the blood was suddenly rushing to Marcus' face and he knew that he was turning red as a beet.

"How about you just worry about your own self?" Marcus asked.

Although his suggestion was anything but pleasant, he noticed that his sister was still smiling to herself, almost as if she knew a secret she was holding inside. Marcus wished that she would keep her thoughts to herself. Truth be told, he'd been looking for a way to ask Lucy Schrock out for the last six years. Marcus had been madly in love with the beautiful, petite girl since they went to the one-room schoolhouse together. Marcus simply wasn't good with talking or romance. Give him a list of figures to work or a farm to tend to and he'd do fine, but he got totally tongue-tied when it came to talking to girls!

Shaking his head to himself, Marcus took in a deep breath. Maybe today would be different. Maybe Annie was right – perhaps it was time for him to step out, take the bull by the horns, and ask Lucy to go with him.

Chapter Two

Jumping down from her seat on the buggy, Annie looked up at her brother before she headed into the small, one-room Amish storehouse.

"Are you coming in or staying out here?"

Marcus shrugged, trying to look uncaring as he muttered, "I haven't decided yet."

Annie couldn't wipe the smirk off her face as she laughed and said, "Well, I'll go on and start getting my stuff."

Sitting on the buggy seat, Marcus looked at his surroundings. To the right was the Schrock's white farm house where he could see Mrs. Schrock hanging laundry on the line. The sight of Lucy's mother made him realize that Lucy would certainly be the one working inside the store.

Gathering all his courage, Marcus stepped down from the buggy seat and worked to tie the horse's reigns to a nearby hitching post. It felt like his fingers were jelly as he tried to make the knot.

Ach! If he couldn't do a simple thing like tie a knot, how could he expect his nerves to handle asking Lucy out on a date?

Taking in a deep breath, he reached for the door to the Amish store and stepped into the dimly lit shed. Shelves of material, yarn, homemade gift items, and supply filled the store.

And there, standing at a wooden counter, was Lucy Schrock.

Marcus grabbed a ball of twine off a nearby shelf and began to absentmindedly roll it around in his hands, trying to look like he was shopping while, actually, he was just observing Lucy from a distance.

She was certainly a beauty in her own, reserved way. Wisps of curly dark hair escaped her *prayer kapp*, framing her thin face. Even though Marcus wasn't close enough to see them, he knew that she had dreamy brown eyes that always looked so gentle and kind – just like her personality. *Ach*, Lucy was one whose beauty went much deeper than just the skin. She was thoughtful and considerate, treating everyone with the same respect and tender care.

She was just the type of girl that a man would want for a wife. It was a surprise that she had stayed single for so long and, if Marcus didn't make his move soon, she would certainly become someone's wife...just not his!

Taking a deep breath, Marcus set the ball of twine aside and collected his courage. Bridging the distance between them, it felt like his shoes were full of led as he made his way to the counter.

Lucy was bent over a ledger, working figures when Marcus reached her side. When he cleared his throat, she looked up from her work and smiled at him.

"Oh, hello there Marcus!" She greeted him, her face lighting up, "How are you today?"

Leaning against the counter, Marcus grabbed for a loose pencil in a ten-cent sale box. Rolling it across his fingers, Marcus cleared his throat again and said, "Oh, I'm doing pretty good. Just working hard. How about yourself?"

Glancing down at her ledger before she looked back up to meet his eyes, Lucy nodded her head, "I'm doing the same."

"Are you...I mean...Sunday...well..." Marcus tried to form the words to ask Lucy to go to the young peoples' singing with him, but it felt like they simply got stuck in his throat.

Lucy leaned forward against the counter, staring at him. Marcus wished that he could just disappear. He looked like such a moron! By this point, he was so embarrassed, he felt like it would be impossible to ever repair his mistake. Even if he could find the nerve and ability to ask her out, he would be too ashamed now! After such a pathetic performance, she would surely not accept his offer.

The sound of the door opening alerted them that someone else had entered the store. Marcus closed his eyes and let out a deep sigh of relief. Thankfully, someone was there who would distract Lucy...and hopefully help her to forget how stupid he had been.

"Well, well!" A familiar voice called out, "I didn't expect to see you here!"

Marcus' eyes got large and he smiled when he realized that the new customer was his older brother, Amos.

"What are you doing?" Marcus asked, still trying to get over his nerves after attempting to talk to Lucy.

Giving a shrug, Amos went up to the counter and smirked, "I just had something I needed to take care of before I went home."

Marcus nodded, "Annie's in here shopping."

"Well, I bet I beat you home."

Amos' statement was rather ridiculous. Since he was still being chauffeured around in his work driver's truck, it was fairly obvious that he would be home first.

Leaning against the counter, Amos said, "Hey there, Lucy. Have you got a minute to talk?"

Looking up at him, Lucy nodded, "Sure. What's up?"

"Sunday night...what are your plans? Would you let me have the honor of driving you to the singing in my buggy?"

Marcus felt his heart drop in his stomach. Surely he wasn't really hearing what it sounded like his brother was saying! As far as he knew, Amos had never liked Lucy or any other girl.

He listened in horror as Lucy replied, "Of course, *jah*! Sure I'll go with you!"

Her voice sounded so excited and hopeful – just as Marcus had envisioned her sounding when *he* asked her out.

Marcus hardly even realized when Annie brought her groceries up to the counter. She started piling up material and yarn, waiting on Lucy to add them up and give her a total. Amos continued to talk, setting up the details of their date.

When Marcus and Annie were safely settled on the buggy seat and well on their way home, Annie finally brought up what had happened.

"What on earth?" She exclaimed, letting out a sigh, "I never would have guessed Amos and Lucy would start dating!"

Marcus sighed and swallowed hard around the lump in his throat. Suddenly, he found himself tongue-tied once again...only this time it wasn't nerves that were stopping his words; instead, it was a heart that felt like it was breaking.

Chapter Three

"So," Amos announced as he spooned some fresh green beans onto his plate, "I had a busy day. I finished up that project at the Sims' house this afternoon and then I headed off to the store and invited Lucy Schrock out on Sunday!"

Marcus tried to swallow the piece of pork chop that he had just put in his mouth. Generally, the Amish young folk were very shy and reserved, keeping who they were dating a secret even from those closest to them. Amos, on the other hand, had never seemed to observe the same rules. Rather than keeping his dates secret, he would always announce them as if he deserved a trophy.

"Oh, what wonderful news!" Their *mamm* smiled broadly at her son's news.

Daed also nodded his head, "Yes, that is great, son. It's been a long time since you've had a date to the singing."

"I don't want to make you feel rushed," *Mamm* continued, passing the mashed potatoes Amos' direction, "But you really should try to make this one work. You're not a child anymore, Amos. You're almost twenty-four-years-old and one of the oldest single men in our community. Lucy is a lovely, lovely girl. She would make any man happy."

Grabbing for his glass of water, Marcus took a big gulp, wishing that he could hurry through this meal and get away to the solitude of his room as soon as possible.

Looking up, he noticed Annie glance at him across the table. Her blue eyes were filled with uncertainty and something akin to sympathy.

"I know Marcus has never had much interest in girls or getting married," Mrs. Christner continued, "But, Amos, you're not like your brother...you should settle down with a good Amish girl and start raising a family."

Pushing his chair back against the hardwood floor, Marcus threw his napkin to the table and announced, "I'm not feeling too well tonight. I'm going on to bed."

There was no way that he could handle any more talk about Lucy and Amos' budding relationship. *Mamm* had no clue how much her words were hurting. Perhaps she was right; maybe Marcus simply wasn't the type to ever have a girlfriend or a family of his own.

Sunday night rolled around much quicker than Marcus would have liked. He hoped to stay home, but his parents were persistent that he should continue to go to the young peoples' meetings. They claimed that, even if he wasn't interested in the attention of a girl, he needed to spend time with others his own age.

With both Annie and Amos out on dates of their own, Marcus found himself traveling alone on his buggy. He spent the entire half-hour ride trying to gather his courage and prepare himself to see his older brother with the girl that he loved.

Despite all of his preparation, as soon as he stepped into the barn where the singing was being held, Marcus felt his heart drop. There were Amos and Lucy sitting side-by-side at a table. He couldn't help but notice the way that her eyes sparkled when she looked up at Amos.

Just seeing it sent a flood of pain through Marcus. How could he be expected to survive a night of watching his life-long crush falling in love with his brother?

"Marcus!" Amos' loud voice rang out across the crowd of people, "Come over here...we've got room over here."

Closing his eyes and gritting his teeth against what was ahead, Marcus made his way through the crowd of Amish young folk until he reached his brother's side. Amos pointed toward a chair and announced, "Take a seat! I was just talking to Lucy about what you're doing on the farm. Now, honest opinion, Marcus, don't you think that I could do as well as you if I just put my mind to it?"

Marcus raised an eyebrow and shrugged before slowly answering as honestly as he could, "*Jah*...I guess you could do anything if you put your mind to it."

"Of course he could!" Lucy interjected, "Amos is a smart fellow...I know he can do anything he wants to!"

Amos grinned and, leaning back in his chair, put his arm across Lucy's shoulders. Watching her beaming face, Marcus felt like he would explode with a mixture of emotions. Having his brother date the girl that he loved was not going to be easy!

Chapter Four

As the weeks passed, watching Amos and Lucy grow closer to one another did not come any easier for Marcus. Week after week, they went to the singing together and Lucy seemed to grow increasingly more in love with Marcus' brother.

The way that things were going, Marcus expected the couple to announce their engagement within the next few months. As old as they were, it seemed that it was certainly time for them to both settle down and start raising a family of their own.

So, it came as a complete surprise one afternoon when Amos came out to the barn to deliver some shocking news.

"I'm breaking up with Lucy."

Marcus felt like his jaw was going to drop completely to the hard-packed dirt floor as he watched his older brother shuffle his black shoes back and forth.

"What?" Marcus couldn't think of anything else to say. The thought of Amos breaking up with Lucy was almost too much to imagine. Although Marcus had been dreaming of this day, now that it had come, it seemed almost sad. He knew from watching Lucy that she had grown incredibly attached to his brother. The idea of Amos just dumping her actually made Marcus feel terrible.

"Amos," Marcus couldn't believe the words that started coming from his lips, "Don't you see how much she cares about you?"

Amos shrugged and nodded his head, "*Jah*...but, Marcus, I just don't feel the same way. Sure, Lucy is a nice girl and you couldn't ask for anyone much more fun...but I don't love her at all. I don't even like her. I'm tired of her. Now, Ruby Miller just moved to the community and she's single. I want a chance with her before the other guys ask her out first...and I can't do that if Lucy is in the way."

Something about Amos' way of talking about Lucy made Marcus irritated. He struggled not to punch his brother in the face.

"Anyway," Amos finished, "I'm going to tell her that things are over. I'm going over to her place here in just a few minutes. But I hate to leave her without a date for the singing Sunday night. Would you be willing to take her?"

Although Marcus had always dreamed of taking Lucy to the young peoples' events, he certainly hadn't expected it to be like this. Shaking his head slowly, he said, "She'll never go along with it..."

"But you're okay if she says yes?"

Stopping to think, Marcus finally shrugged and said, "Sure. *Jah*...if she says yes, then I'll take her."

Marcus was fairly certain that was one thing that would not be happening!

To Marcus' surprise, Sunday night found him on his way to pick up Lucy Schrock. Completely knocking him off his feet, Lucy accepted the invitation for him to take her to the young people's gathering.

Marcus couldn't decide why Lucy had agreed to go to the singing with him. A small part of his heart hoped that she had secret feelings for him but, in all honesty, that seemed unlikely. After seeing the looks that Lucy shared with his brother, Marcus was fairly certain that she was struck on Amos wholeheartedly.

Pulling his buggy up to Lucy's house, Marcus waited anxiously as he twisted the horse's reigns around in his hands.

Lucy came rushing out of the house, working to tie her black bonnet in place.

"Hello there Marcus," She greeted, her voice sounding rather curt and strained as she hurried to pull herself onto the wooden seat beside him, "How are you tonight?"

Marcus nodded, so confused that he didn't even feel nervous, "I'm good. How about yourself?"

Lucy didn't really answer; instead, she simply gave a shrug.

They started down the road without another word said between them. Marcus wasn't sure whether he should try to bring up a pleasant topic to talk about or simply let the conversation stay dead.

Finally, Lucy cleared her throat and sat up straighter in her seat, "Marcus...you probably wonder why I let you drive me tonight. To be honest, a part of me wishes that I'd just stayed home. But I love your brother. Amos has grown to mean so much to me over the past few weeks...I'm not just going to sit back and let him walk away without trying to fight for him."

Marcus hoped she didn't notice him roll his eyes as he tried to bite his tongue and keep his words in check. After all that Amos had done to Lucy, the last thing she should do was worry about getting him back.

"He said there was someone else," Lucy announced, her voice trembling as she forced the question out, "Do you know who she is?"

Before he could stop himself, the name popped out of Marcus' mouth, "It's that new girl, Ruby Miller."

Out of the corner of his eye, Marcus watched Lucy's face go white and she slowly nodded her head, "Ruby's sure mighty pretty."

Not as pretty as you, Marcus wanted to say, but instead he kept silent.

"Marcus," Lucy bit down on her lip, obviously trying to formulate her words, "I know that you've never been one to have a girlfriend. You've always been so busy with your work that you haven't had time for a relationship. But, right now, I need your help. I want to be able to keep showing up around Amos so that, when he gets tired of Ruby, he'll come back to me. Would you consider taking me to singings and doing things with me? I'm not asking you to be my boyfriend or anything like that...I'm just asking you to pretend. It won't take a whole lot of your time and I won't expect much. Will you think about it?"

Would he think about it? Marcus wouldn't have to think about it! He was tempted to tell Lucy that he wanted to go out with her for himself, that he had always loved her, but the words got stuck in his throat. Instead, he just nodded and replied, "I think I can do that."

Sitting back against the seat, Lucy gave a satisfied nod of her head.

Marcus wasn't sure what was ahead with this fake relationship but he knew one thing – at least this would give him a chance to get to know this beautiful girl. Who could tell what would happen? Maybe she'd end up falling in love with him after all!

Chapter Five

If Marcus hadn't known that his "date" with Lucy was simply a front for her to stay close to Amos, it would almost have been a dream come true. Although things were somewhat strained between them, as the night progressed, Lucy began to ask him questions about his work and genuinely seemed to take an interest in the things that he did.

Amos obviously saw that things were going well, because he led his date over to the bench where Lucy and Marcus were sitting, and plopped down right beside Marcus with his new girlfriend, Ruby, at his side. Marcus couldn't keep from grimacing as he felt Lucy bristle.

"So, you farm all of that land," Lucy announced, her voice rising in obvious hopes that Amos would hear her, "All by yourself. That is amazing, Marcus! Could I come out to your house and see it tomorrow?"

Although Marcus knew that it was simply another ploy to get back together with his brother, he couldn't keep from feeling a spark of excitement at the thought of Lucy coming to see the farm of which he was so proud. Nodding his head, he tried to remind himself that he shouldn't get too hopeful or excited about anything they did together.

The next afternoon, Marcus picked Lucy up in his buggy and gave her a ride out to his farm.

"I thought I ought to tell you," Marcus announced before Lucy could even get seated, "Amos isn't going to be home until later today. He ended up going to work with the construction crew."

Lucy's smile instantly fell. She frowned and looked at Marcus as if she was considering her options.

"You don't have to come with me, if you don't want to." Marcus replied, "We can wait until a different day when Amos will be home."

To Marcus' total surprise, Lucy shook her head and said, "No...I'll come anyway. I'd like to see your place. If you don't mind, that is."

Marcus and Lucy spent a lovely afternoon together as she traveled across his acres of land, talking with him about all that he had accomplished and the ways that he had managed to increase his profits every year.

As he spent time with her, Marcus remembered why he had always been attracted to Lucy. She was simply a joy to be around. Lucy Schrock was thoughtful, kind, gentle, and genuinely interested in the things that she asked.

It was hard for Marcus to imagine why Amos would ever consider a different girl when he had the opportunity to spend his life with Lucy.

That one day wasn't the only that they spent together. Over the next few months, Marcus and Lucy continued to do many things together. From picnics to young peoples' meetings, the summer months slowly drifted away into the fall.

One chilly September afternoon, Marcus picked Lucy up to take her to a community picnic held at the Hostetler family's barn. Lucy seemed more talkative than even usual, explaining what was going on with the store and about a new cleaning job she had recently started.

"I'm beginning to wonder about Amos," Lucy finally sighed as she sucked in a breath of cool air and shook her head, "I never thought that he and Ruby would last, but they certainly seem to be enjoying each other's company."

And Marcus was certainly enjoying the time that he got to spend with her. Looking down at his hands, he managed to ask, "Are you pretty much miserable all the time now?"

Lucy cocked her head to one side in thoughtful contemplation as they made their way down the quiet country road.

"No, I'm not miserable," she finally announced, "I mean, I haven't totally given up hope that things will change with Amos. He might still realize that he has feelings for me...but it just seems unlikely. On the other hand, I truly have had a *gut* summer...thanks to you, Marcus."

Turning to look in her eyes, Marcus wanted to say something, anything that would make her realize how he felt about her. Instead, he simply went numb, the words in his mind jumbling together before he could get them out.

Chapter Six

"Where are you off to?" The voice of Marcus' sister, Annie, interrupted his thoughts as he reached for his hat and put it on his head, "Going to see your sweetheart, perhaps?"

Marcus felt his face grow red at his little sister's teasing. Looking around the house and thankful to realize that it was empty, Marcus stepped up close to the sink where Annie was busy washing lunch dishes.

"I'm going out to the barn to work some on calf pens for *Daed*," Marcus replied firmly, "And Lucy is *not* my girlfriend."

While Marcus was keeping the entire situation with Lucy a secret from the rest of his family, he had confided her plans with Annie.

Looking up at him, Annie sighed and shook her head, "*Ach*, Marcus. Are you and she still keeping up with that silly plan? That's such a joke! Why don't you just tell her that you love her and allow yourself some happiness?"

Marcus shook his head as he reached out to put his finger in his sister's dishwater, "It's not that simple..."

"*Jah* – it is!" Annie insisted as she ran a dishcloth across one of their plain white plates, "Lucy loves you. I can see it in her eyes every time that she looks at you. But this holding off is crazy. She may not realize how much she cares but maybe, if you would just open up your heart to her, she'd open hers up to you!"

Marcus rolled his eyes, wishing that his well-meaning sister would simply stop, "You don't know a thing about it, Annie. You don't know how hard this is on me."

Turning to face him, Annie put her soapy hands on her hips, not even caring that they got her dress wet, "I'll tell you what I know, Marcus Christner! I know that Amos has fallen head-over-heels for that Ruby girl, and he will never look at Lucy Schrock again. I also know that you'll never be happy if Lucy isn't in your life. And Lucy is never going to find a man that she enjoys as much as she likes being around you. I don't care how smitten she was with our older brother...it's you she actually wants to spend time around!"

Hearing Annie's words put more hope in Marcus' heart than he wanted to admit. Growing bashful, he reached up and put his hand on his face, trying to hide his embarrassment.

"Marcus..." Annie's voice softened, "Have ya ever thought that maybe God put you in this situation for a reason? He's involved in every part of life, Marcus. Maybe He set things up so that you'd have a chance to get to know Lucy and tell her how you feel about her!"

Standing up straighter, Marcus announced, "I'm going out to the barn."

With that, he turned and left the house. As he walked out to the barn, Annie's words kept playing through his mind over and over again.

What if she was right? What if God had finally answered his prayers about Lucy? What if He had brought Lucy into this spot so that Marcus would have the chance to talk to her?

Marcus shook his head. He just wasn't sure that he would ever have the courage to tell Lucy how he felt.

Chapter Seven

Sunday morning Marcus sat in church, trying not to think about his troubles with Lucy. The more time that they spent together, the closer he felt to her and the more love he knew was growing in his heart. At times, Marcus felt that the struggle of loving Lucy and knowing she only had eyes for his brother was more than he could handle.

Marcus hated to admit it, but he hardly heard a word that was said during the entire church service. All he could do was try to fight off his miserable thoughts.

"Before we go outside for our community lunch, someone wants to make an announcement," Preacher Joe told everyone before they could stand up when the service came to a close.

To Marcus' total surprise, Amos stood up along with Ruby Miller. Looking from one to the other, Marcus could see that they were both beaming with excitement.

"Amos Christner comes forward to announce that he will be marrying Ruby Miller in two weeks," Preacher Joe continued, his own face breaking out in a big smile.

Marcus' gaze immediately went to Lucy. She was sitting on the bench with the other Amish women, her face completely ashen and her eyes large. Marcus' heart broke for her. He couldn't imagine how much pain she was feeling.

As the service came to a close, Marcus grabbed his felt hat and stood to his feet. Before he could start for the door, Lucy came to his side and pulled on his sleeve.

"Marcus," she said, her voice little more than a whisper, "I'm not feeling well. Can you please drive me home?"

If Marcus didn't tell her 'yes', then she would be forced to stay and endure the entire meal with the community until her family was ready to leave.

Marcus nodded his head. It was the least that he could do.

The buggy ride home from church was long and miserable. Lucy hardly said a word –she just sat in stunned silence, letting out an occasional shudder.

When they reached her empty house and both got down from the buggy, Lucy finally found the courage to speak.

"I can't believe that they're getting married," Lucy whispered under her breath, tears beginning to form in her eyes, "I just can't believe it. There go all my hopes and dreams of a family of my own."

"Now, Lucy, things aren't like that at all..."

"Yes, they are." Lucy interrupted Marcus before he could continue, "I'm the oldest girl in our community. Amos is one of the only single men. I don't know what's wrong with me that men don't like me, but it just seems like I'm destined to be an old maid."

Reaching up to wipe tears away from her eyes, Lucy admitted, "*Ach*, Marcus. I don't know...these weeks with you have made me think that I didn't actually like Amos so much after all. I mean, maybe I didn't like him as much as I just liked the idea of having a boyfriend." Shaking her head, Lucy looked up to meet Marcus, her eyes filled with tears that were beginning to spill down her cheeks.

"Thank you, Marcus," she whispered, her voice getting choked up, "Thank you for all that you did to try to be there for me. Thank you for taking me out on dates and doing things with me. I know that it must have been a burden on you and I know that you would have rather been working during that time. But it did mean a lot to me. And, honestly," she looked down at her feet and took in a deep breath, "Honestly, Marcus, if you ever decide that you want to settle down, any girl would be lucky to have you. You are truly a prize."

Smiling sadly, she turned and started to walk away.

Marcus felt like all the words he wanted to say were getting stuck in his throat. He just stood there, like an idiot, watching as she made her way toward her house.

He couldn't let her go. He just couldn't!

Breathing a quick prayer for strength, Marcus gathered his courage and took off after her.

"Lucy! Lucy, wait!" He exclaimed, reaching out to grab her by the elbow and turning her so that she was looking into his eyes.

"Listen here, Lucy!" Marcus announced, "I want you to hear something and I want you to understand. I love you. I always have. From the time that we were in school together, you've been the only girl who ever caught my eye. You're sweet and kind...and so brave...and you are smart about so many things. And you're a thousand times prettier than Ruby Miller or any other girl on the face of this planet. You mean everything to me, Lucy. And, although it's mean, I'm glad Amos doesn't want you back...I'm glad because I want you!

As soon as the words escaped his lips, Lucy's jaw dropped and her eyes got huge. Marcus wondered if he had made a bad decision to pursue her. Perhaps he should have just let her go without another word. Growing instantly bashful, Marcus looked down at his feet, "I mean...that is...well, I don't know..."

"Marcus," Lucy's voice sounded so small, "Marcus, I can't believe it." Reaching out to put her hand in his, she explained, "During our time together, I have fallen in love with you as well. I have always cared about you, but it seemed ridiculous since you were so wrapped up in your work. I thought that you just wanted to be an old bachelor for the rest of your life."

Looking up to meet her eyes, Marcus couldn't believe what he was hearing.

"So...you actually...like me?"

Lucy nodded, a broad smile crossing her face, "Yes, Marcus, I actually like you. And do you actually like me?"

Rather than answering her silly question, Marcus leaned down and showed her by planting a tender kiss on her lips. Pulling her tight against him in a hug, he breathed in the fresh scent of her hair through her *prayer kapp* and closed his eyes.

Finally, Marcus had found the happiness he had always wanted.

AMISH DREAMS

MONICA MARKS

"Where did you ever learn to make such delicious bread?" he murmured in her ear, his lips grazing the top of her ear. Delicious shivers coursed down her spine and she turned to face him, her heart filled with adulation.

"I don't know," she replied, her blue eyes glowing. *"Where did you learn to be such a wonderful husband?"*

He deposited a soft kiss on her rosebud lips and smiled warmly, his brown eyes twinkling mischievously.

"Maybe I am part Amish," he joked and she chuckled, turning back to turn off the oven. His cell phone chimed and he released her waist to look at it.

"Oh," he muttered, a perplexed look crossing over his face. *"I have to go back to the office."*

"At this hour? You just returned home!" she protested but he was already at the door.

"I will be back as soon as I can. A client needs me. I can't say no," he told her, blowing her a kiss. *"I love you."*

"I love you too," she sighed as the door closed in her husband's wake. She looked at the dinner she had spent hours making and flopped onto a chair, defeated.

I guess I'm eating alone again tonight, she thought, sadly.

"Honor! You are burning the bread!"

Charity jumped ahead of her sister, reaching into the oven to retrieve the loaves from the heat within. Honor stood back, watching blankly as Charity rescued the crusty dough and dropped them on the counter, her brow furrowed slightly. She righted the bread and turned to face her older sister, wiping her hands on her apron.

"Are you unwell?" she demanded but Charity already knew the answer to her own question. Honor had been unwell for months. She might never be well again but Charity refused to acknowledge any of those thoughts.

She made a bad decision but she is home now and in time, God will help her through the pain she is feeling.

Honor sat on a stool behind the counter and placed her head in her hands, without responding. Her soft blue eyes were shadowed with sorrow and Charity could not help but feel sympathy for her sister. She climbed on the stool at Honor's side and gently stroked her back.

"Honor, it has been three months. It is time to let go," she said quietly and Honor looked at her younger sister, her mouth pulled into a frown. Tears glistened in her eyes.

"Don't you think I want to put that part of my life in the past, Charity?" she retorted, her voice choked with emotion. "I do not wish to wake up every morning with tears streaking my pillow or toss and turn the night away, longing for my husband's embrace."

"Ex-husband," Charity mumbled and Honor's spine stiffened. She pushed Charity's arm from her body and stood.

"Yes. Ex-husband. Thank you for reminding me," she growled, storming from the bakery and leaving Charity to regret opening her mouth.

"Duncan, are you going out?"

Honor stared at him as she entered the bedroom from the master bathroom, her face freshly washed. Her husband was dressed in a suit, freshly showered and shaved, looking incredibly handsome.

He flashed her a small smile, slipping his watch onto his wrist and slipped over to kiss her on her cheek.

"I just had a client fly in from out of town," he told her as her nostrils filled with the scent of his spicy cologne. "I have to go talk to him about some papers he needs to sign."

"Can it not wait until morning?" Honor implored beseechingly, turning her wide eyes on him. He shifted his gaze, from her and adjusted his jacket in the mirror. She could not understand why his clients were constantly arriving at odd times of night, needing to sign off on papers and take my husband away. I should have married an accountant. Lawyers are far too consumed with their work.

"I'm afraid it can't, honey. I won't be terribly long but don't wait up, okay?"

Honor watched as he disappeared and tried not to notice that he had left his wedding ring on the dresser again.

"Honor, we have spoken the bishop about having you baptized in October."

Honor glanced up at her father uncomprehendingly. His words sent consternation through her spine and her immediate response was indignation.

"Were you going to speak with me about this decision or have I no say in this?" she retorted, dropping her fork onto the table with a clang. Her family raised their eyes in stunned surprised. The youngest went pale, looking at one another, unsure of how to react.

"Honor, we assumed that you came home because you wished to be with united with the community again," Isaac Fisher replied slowly, also lowering his utensils to his plate and staring at his second oldest child. Honor pursed her lips and stared at her plate, ashamed at her outburst.

I have no right for being upset with father for assuming I am getting baptized. Why does this anger you so much? He is only watching out for your best interests. You are blessed to have someone still willing to do that after the mess you made.

"I am sorry, *Daed*," she whispered. "Of course that Is fine."

Isaac's light eyes narrowed slightly and he glanced at his wife who looked just as confused as him. Rachel Fisher fixed her eyes on the table and waited for her husband to speak with his unnaturally irate daughter. He cleared his throat as if choosing his words selectively. He understood that Honor was in a fragile state and he did not wish to further poke at the bear with his questions but if she was to be baptized, arrangements needed to be made.

"That is fine then. You will be required to attend your meetings with the ministers and the deacon in preparation."

"Of course, *Daed*," Honor replied. She picked up her fork and continued to eat as her siblings began to chatter quietly among themselves.

They are ignoring my blathering as if I am mad. They are worried they will say or do something to cause me to overreact again, Honor thought mournfully as her siblings avoided eye contact with her.

She was embarrassed at her behavior. When she had left the district behind for Indianapolis, her parents had been upset but understanding. When she had eloped with Duncan three months later, they had been devastated but they had maintained their compassionate way, never making her feel as if she had done wrong. Even when she had come home, heartbroken and divorced, they had never faltered in their support of her, despite the backlash her return had caused in the district.

"Dat, you and Mammi have exercised so much mercy toward me. How can you continue to love and stand by me despite my awful choices?" Honor had asked, her face soaked with tears of regret.

"God gave you free will, Honor. You will return to us if you are meant to be here, if your faith is pure. If it is not, you must find your way somewhere where you are happy. All we have ever wanted for our children is their happiness," Isaac had told her after her divorce.

"I am meant to be here," she had cried, wiping at her streaked cheeks. "I am sorry I caused you any pain."

"No, child," her father had replied, stroking her hair lovingly. "We are sorry you are feeling pain. The only pain we feel is when you hurt, Honor."

I will get baptized in the autumn and forget I ever made such a foolish decision, Honor told herself. *It is the right thing to do. You have caused your family enough shame and worry, no matter what father says. They should not have to bear the burden of your poor choices.*

Honor took a sip of water and looked about the table of the family whom she loved dearly, her eyes meeting Charity's briefly. The sisters exchanged a look and Honor looked down, swallowing the rock in her throat.

You will do it, not because you wish to be baptized but because it is the proper thing to do. Your needs no longer matter when you have done so much wrong.

"Honor, you needn't be at the bakery every day," Charity told her sister as they rode the buggy into town toward their family's shop. "I have been handling it just fine before you came home."

A flash of guilt sparked through Honor and she looked at her younger sister quickly. They were only eighteen months apart and of all six of the siblings, likely the closest. They were often mistaken for twins, the only two of the Fisher children with ash blonde hair and bright blue eyes. Their features were unmistakably that of their mother with high, regal cheekbones and a strong, bold jaw.

When Honor had gone to Indianapolis, she had missed Charity terribly. They had written one another often and Charity had made the trip to Indianapolis once but she had cut her trip short, uncomfortable with the hustle of the big city, staying only one night.

When Honor had returned home, seeing Charity's bright face had lifted Honor's broken spirit considerably.

"More the reason for me to help now," Honor replied lightly. "I must catch up for lost time. Perhaps it is you who should stay behind and allow for me to work the bakery alone."

Charity smirked slightly.

"And who would deal with the customers while you are hiding away in the kitchen?" Charity asked. Honor felt herself tense slightly. She peered at her sister, trying to hide her anger.

"Would you rather I stayed behind with Mam on the farm?" she asked tersely and Charity shook her head.

"No, Honor. I am happy to have the company. I would rather you spend the time healing than working."

"I am healed," Honor protested but she heard the weakness in her words. Charity shook her head and urged the horse forward as they approached town.

As they entered the Arthur city limits, Charity frowned slightly.

"Oh, they are doing construction on the old theater on South Maple," she commented. Honor craned her neck to look where her sister was pointing. As Charity had said, there were several men pulling out drywall and tools from three white pick up trucks and into the long-abandoned theater two doors down from the Fisher Bakery. The sisters exchanged a curious glance.

"The English will be happy with that. There is little in Arthur to entertain them without it. It is high time they did something with the space. I wonder who bought it," Honor said as the sisters drew closer. She had not heard news of anyone purchasing the building but she had not genuinely been paying attention. In truth, she had tried to avoid her contact with the English community, despite her role in the bakery. Charity had not been exaggerating when she stated that Honor hid in the back. She had busied herself with the baking, leaving Charity to tend to the customers.

"I haven't heard anything about it," Charity replied, as they finally stopped by the bakery. Honor gathered her long dress and stepped off the cart, glancing skyward, one hand on her white prayer bonnet. Dark clouds were beginning to blot out the early morning sunshine and there was the scent of ozone in the air.

"It looks like rain," she said but Charity had already gone to unlock the shop. Honor followed her sister and the two women spent the morning preparing for the day ahead.

"Where were you all night?" Honor cried, her eyes red-rimmed from tears. Duncan tossed her a casual look and threw his keys on the kitchen table.

"Out," he answered flippantly, undoing his tie. He barely looked at her again as he kicked off his shoes and began to strip out of his clothes.

"Duncan, please talk to me!" Honor pleaded, trailing after him. Tears began to spill down her cheeks. She could not understand what had happened. A month earlier they had been inseparable, snuggling, talking, preparing for the future. Suddenly, they barely said a word to one another, Honor hoping to simply catch a glimpse of her increasingly busy husband most days.

When did I lose him? He was so loving, so attentive. Now he won't even come home at night. What happened? How can I get us back to how we were a few months ago?

He was in his underwear, about to close the bathroom door as the steam from the shower streamed into the master bedroom.

"Honor, don't get hysterical. It's tacky," he sighed, trying to shut the wood but Honor stuck her foot in the door, determined to get answers. She could not live without knowing where Duncan went at night.

"You owe me an explanation," she insisted, forcing back her tears. "You cannot expect me not to wonder where you are night after night, Duncan."

He peered at her for a moment, his mouth turning down into a grimace. At first, she thought he was simply about to block her out yet again but she watched with relief as he opened his mouth to respond for once.

"I thought you would be different than other women," he muttered, standing back and folding his arms. "I thought because of your background, you wouldn't be a nagging shrew but I can see I was wrong. I suppose women everywhere are the same. It's in your nature."

Honor stepped back, shocked at the cruelty of his words.

Nagging shrew? Wondering where my husband goes at night makes me a nagging shrew? She wondered, flabbergasted. Who is this man and where is the man I married?

She could not bring herself to protest his assessment, staring at him in stunned silence.

"You want to know where I am at night? I am with another woman, one who doesn't cry and whine when I see her. Can you blame me?" He slammed the door, leaving Honor to gape after him in shock.

He left again that night and she did not see him again, the divorce papers arriving via courier two days later. He refused to answer his phone or take her calls at the office and when she went to his work, she was always told he was not there.

She had been torn between wanting to fall into a sobbing mess of histrionics and quietly disappearing. All she wanted was to talk to Duncan, truly talk to him so they could discuss what had happened but he was determined to avoid her.

Honor finally had no choice but to sign the papers, seeing her husband only one more time, in court as they finalized their divorce. By that time, she had no more words, not understanding how she could have fallen so foolishly for a man she barely knew. She felt nothing but deep shame for what she had allowed to happen.

Honor willingly left the apartment which had been in Duncan's name and returned home to her family who had welcomed her as if she had never left. The thought of staying in the city had not crossed her mind. She wished to return home where she could relish in the seclusion. And she vowed to never give up her heart to anyone ever again.

"Hello?"

Someone was calling out from the front of the bakery and Honor waited for Charity to attend to the customer, her hands covered in flour as she rolled dough into small buns.

"Hello? Anyone here?" the man called again and Honor turned her head to catch a glimpse of whomever it was.

"One moment!" she called back, idly wondering where her sister had gone but she didn't fret. It was not uncommon for Charity to get distracted speaking with the town folk on the sidewalk on slower days. That day certainly qualified as did most days. Arthur was hardly the hub of activity on its busiest days.

Honor wiped her hands on her apron and hurried out to greet the customer. She was taken aback for a moment at the stranger in her midst. She prided herself on knowing the people of Arthur. It was only a town of two thousand after all but she did not know the dust and paint splattered man standing on the tile floor opposite the counter.

He looked up at her and she found her breath catch in her throat. His eyes were a dazzling array of colors, a combination of blues, greens and yellows. Honor was certain she had never seen such beautiful eyes.

He held her gaze and she suddenly became aware of it, clearing her throat nervously as she approached the cash register.

"May I help you?" she asked. To her embarrassment, her voice squeaked slightly.

"Uh...yeah..." he replied slowly, still watching her. "Do you have coffee here?"

Honor glanced back at the pot and realized it was empty.

"I can put on a fresh pot," she told him. "If you can wait."

"Well I can't go back there without caffeine," he replied lightly, thrusting his thumb toward the exit. "Or I won't come out alive."

Honor nodded quickly and turned to start the percolator.

"You are working on the theater?" she asked. She was surprised to hear herself asking the question. She had gone out of her way to avoid contact with the customers, especially the Englishers but she found herself striking up a conversation with this man.

He is new in town. It is impolite to not make him feel welcome, she told herself but something in the back of her mind told her that she was being more than merely welcoming. She shrugged off the inane thought and turned back to face him.

"Yeah, my crew and me just started in there. It's a big job. Probably three months, maybe longer."

"That long?" Honor asked, her eyes widening. "What needs to be done?"

"The new owners want it completely gutted. Putting in marble flooring, new walls but they want to keep the original woodworking where they can. That theater dates back to 1890."

Of course, Honor had already known that; she had been born and raised in the Arthur area as had her father and his father before him. There was very little she did not know about the town or its buildings. Yet she shook her head admiringly, her eyes trained on this rugged, handsome face.

"Really?" she answered and he suddenly looked embarrassed.

"I guess you know the history of this town better than I do," he said, abashed but Honor shook her head.

"I know more of the Amish way than that of the English," she answered magnanimously. "I am always interested to learn new things."

She asked herself why she was blatantly lying to this man as if she had something to prove to him.

You are acting like a dim-witted fool, she chided herself but she could not stop smiling at him.

He grinned easily and Honor was sure she had never seen a more disarming sight.

"Well in that case, did you know that the theater is haunted?"

A faint smile flew over her lips but before she could respond, the door to the bakery opened and Charity entered.

"My apologies," she gasped, hurrying behind the counter. "I ran into the Minister Lapp on the street and we began to discuss your baptism."

She smiled charmingly at the stranger.

"I can help you," Charity told him, shooting her sister a meaningful glance. She knew how little a desire Honor had for dealing with people those days. To Charity's surprise Honor shook her head.

"No, it is fine, Charity. We were merely waiting for the coffee to finish which I believe it has now," Honor replied, looking at the now full pot. "How many coffees shall I make?"

"Five, please," the man said. "Charity. That's a pretty name."

Charity beamed chastely and glanced at her sister.

"Our parents named us for the virtues for which they wished us to possess," she answered. "There is Justice, Verity, Hope, Prudence and this here is Honor."

Honor placed the hot paper cups in a tray and produced some creamers and sugar in a bag with stir sticks.

"Honor," he mumbled. "That is somehow fitting of you."

Her head turned at the words, a spark of electricity shocking her and their eyes met again.

If only that was true, Honor thought, suddenly losing the short-lived happiness this stranger had caused her. *My honor is besmirched, soiled.*

He blushed crimson and reached in his work stained pants for money.

"Ah, how much do I owe you?" he asked, seemingly nervous.

"Seven fifty," Charity piped up and Honor could hear a sly note in her voice. Honor dared not look at her sister, hanging her head as a sudden shame overcame her.

How utterly ridiculous you just behaved, Honor chided herself, stepping toward the back or the store as the workman handed Charity a crumpled bill.

"Good bye," Honor muttered, hurrying back into the kitchen but not before she heard her sister speak again.

"You know our names but we don't know yours," she said pleasantly. Honor found herself pausing to hear the answer.

"Drew. Drew Harrington."

"Wait, Audra, don't hang up!"

It was too late. The blank screen on his cell told him that she had done precisely that. Frustrated, he whipped the phone at the ground and stared in dismay as it shattered into a hundred pieces. He was instantly regretful.

This is what she's talking about. This is the reason she left you. You can't react like this, he told himself but the feeling of loss and desperation was overwhelming. He wanted to scream and cry and punch a wall.

He looked at the tattered remains of his handheld device and hung his head in his hands. She was never coming back. They were too far gone, too much had happened and he had handled it so poorly.

He slowly leaned forward and picked up the phone, trying to put it back together.

That's what I've been doing for over a year now. Trying to put something back together that is broken beyond repair. You can call her from a dozen different numbers and beg her in a million different tones. The love we once shared died a year ago on March 15th. It is time to move on and let Audra move on too.

"Did you go to Columbia and pick the beans?" the foreman yelled as Drew returned to the theater with the tray of coffee in hand. "Because it better taste like it!"

Drew grunted and set the beverages down on a pile of debris, watching as his coworkers came flocking to the intoxicating scent of caffeine.

"Did you go next door to that little Amish bakery?" Mike asked and Drew nodded.

"I went in there once last week. Cute girl running that place," he commented. "I always thought those people hated us outsiders but she was really nice to me."

"Honor?" Drew asked before he could stop himself. He cringed, ready for a ribbing from the boys but Mike's brow furrowed.

"No, Charity. Who is Honor?"

"That's the sister who never comes out of the back. Rumor in town is that she ran off and married one of us and got a divorce," Brian piped up, taking a sip of his cup. "Did you meet her, Drew?"

Drew was stunned by the revelation.

"Who told you that?" Drew demanded. Brian laughed.

"There are like twelve people in this town, Drew. They have nothing to do but gossip."

"Can they do that? Marry outside their community?" Drew asked. He didn't claim to know the first thing about Amish culture except that they were close-knit and lived by a separate code than the rest of America. Brian shrugged indifferently.

"I guess so because she did."

I guess I'm not the only one with skeletons in my closet, Drew thought, pushing Audra from his mind and replacing his former wife's face with that of the beautiful girl next door.

"You have a meeting with the deacon this afternoon, Honor," Isaac reminded his daughter as she cleared the dishes from breakfast. She cast him a sidelong look but did not reply.

"Honor?" her father asked. "Did you remember?"

She piled the plates nervously on her arm and nodded.

"Yes, *Daed*," she replied. It had been weighing heavily on her mind for days but the thought of talking to the elders in preparation for her baptism was causing a ball of stress in the pit of her belly. She could not explain her apprehension.

That is categorically untrue. You know exactly why you are so ill at ease; you are not certain you wish to be baptized.

"Honor, is there something you would like to discuss?" Isaac asked gently. "Are you troubled?"

"No, *Daed*," she replied honestly. She most certainly did not wish to discuss her worries with her father. She did not want him to know that she had been looking forward to the daily visits from the Englisher working in the theater. It was bad enough that Charity could see her mounting affection for the hardworking soul. She could not devastate her family again with more foolishness.

"I will be there," she promised her father, offering him a quick smile before disappearing into the kitchen with the stack of plates. Honor's parents exchanged a look of nervousness. Something was not right with their daughter and they knew it.

The bell chimed at the front of the store and Charity wiped her hands, prepared to see to the customer but Honor stopped her.

"I'll get it," she chirped. She returned a moment later, a slightly disappointed expression on her face.

"Wasn't who you were expecting?" Charity asked dryly. Honor's eyes narrowed.

"It was Mrs. Tilly. She wanted a dozen rolls."

"So, no, not who you were expecting," Charity answered. Honor did not answer, knowing what her sister was implying.

"Do you remember when I came to visit you in Indianapolis?" Charity asked, very much off topic. Honor nodded slowly, raising her eyes from the muffins she was setting in trays.

"Of course. You stayed but a day."

"I did not like Duncan from the moment I laid eyes upon him," Charity said conversationally and Honor felt herself tensing. Charity noticed and continued speaking.

"This is not a testament to you, Honor. There was simply something about him which I found distasteful. It had nothing to do with you leaving or marrying so quickly. You may call it intuition or a warning from God but I could tell there was something not proper about him."

"That is why you left so quickly," Honor finished, trying to keep the sourness from her voice. Charity shook her head.

"No. I had every intention of staying the week but that first night, you went to take a shower and your new husband tried to kiss me."

Shocked, Honor stared at her sister, her mouth agape. Tears filled her eyes.

"Why did you not tell me?" she gasped, her throat filling with bile and fury toward her ex-husband.

"What good would that have done? I knew you would discover what a pitiful creature he was in due time. It was not my place to show you. Anyway, if I had said something, it would only have served to cause a riff in our relationship. You were so in love with Duncan and you already believed that we were angry at you for leaving the community."

Honor could not stop the tears from slipping down her cheeks as she watched Charity nonchalantly knead bread.

"We have only ever wanted you to be happy, Honor. If that means you are to be happy with an Englisher outside of the community, so be it."

The bell chimed at the front of the store but neither women moved.

"Why are you telling me this now?" Honor asked, wiping the tears from her face. Charity smiled softly, finally meeting her sister's eyes.

"Because I don't have a single bad feeling about Drew."

"Hello? Honor?" Drew called from the front of the store. Charity motioned her head.

"Go on. He's calling you," she urged. Honor cleared her throat and dried her eyes.

"I'll be right out," she replied. As she turned toward the front of the store, she wondered if her sister was right.

Will Mam and Daed forgive me if I fall for yet another Englisher? She had no way of knowing for certain.

"I'm leaving, Drew," she said flatly, snapping the clasps of the suitcase closed and yanking it off the bed. "I can't live with you anymore."

He watched her, unable to speak with a thousand words of protest echoing through his mind.

"Ever since we lost the baby, your temper has been out of control. I needed comfort and you needed to release your pain. We have fallen completely apart in the last year and there is no going back."

"Audra, I'm sorry," he whispered, tears in his eyes and she nodded.

"I'm sorry too," she replied, opening the front door. "Good bye, Drew."

"What are you smiling about?" Mike demanded. "You know, I pay you to work not flirt with the Amish twins all day."

"They aren't twins. They're eighteen months apart," Drew replied and the men laughed.

"You have the entire genealogy down over there, huh?" Brian joked. "Are you thinking of converting?"

"They would never take Drew," Mike retorted. "He's divorced."

"So is the older one," Brian reminded him and the men began making "ooh" noises at him. To his surprise, Drew found he was not annoyed by the banter. More and more he was consumed with the idea of asking Honor Fisher on a date.

Would she laugh in my face or consider it? He wondered. Every day when he walked into the bakery, he vowed it would be the day when he would finally build up the courage to do it yet another day passed and he did not.

She already had a bad experience with one man outside her faith. She is probably in no rush to do it again, he reasoned but he could not get the thought of her fair skin and bright eyes out of his mind.

Tomorrow, he told himself. *Tomorrow I will ask her out on a proper date.*

But he wondered if he had changed from the man Audra had left behind two years prior. He hoped so.

"What is this?" Honor asked, slowly walking into the front room. Her entire family had gathered and was watching her expectantly.

"Come in, Honor," Isaac told her. Obediently, Honor crossed over the threshold of the living area and joined her five siblings and her parents. She glanced panicked at Charity who averted her blue eyes and Honor suddenly found it difficult to breathe.

Oh no, Charity, what did you tell them? She found herself wondering.

"Sit down, *liebchen,*" Isaac implored, pointing at a straight back chair near the dining room. Swallowing, Honor sat.

"Honor, Charity tells me you have feelings for a man you met in town," Isaac announced without preamble. Immediately, denial sprung to her lips but died there as she stared at the loving face of her father.

You must not lie to him, she told herself. *Your relationship is based on trust and loyalty. They have never forsaken you, not when many families would have turned their backs on their child for doing what you did.*

"I would not say I have feelings for him, *Daed,*" Honor answered truthfully. "I have only just met the man. I do not know much about him."

"Tell us about him," Isaac responded. Honor looked at Charity again and this time her sister gave her an encouraging nod.

"He...he is a tradesman working on the old theater," she started. "He comes into the bakery every day for coffee."

"What is his name?" Justice demanded, rolling his brown eyes. The other children laughed and Honor felt herself relaxing slightly.

This is not a trial. They are sincerely asking about Drew.

"His name is Drew Harrington."

"That is a strong name," Isaac told her approvingly. Her mother nodded in agreement.

"How does he feel about you, Honor?" Isaac wanted to know. Honor blinked. She had no answer. While she suspected that Drew only came in day after day to spend time with her, she had no way of knowing if he saw her as an amusing pastime or if he sincerely had any feelings toward her.

"He adores her, *Daed,*" Charity replied. Honor looked at her in surprise.

"How can you know that, Charity?" their mother asked reprovingly but the younger sister smiled.

"Because the only other time I have seen a man look at a woman that way is when *Daed* looks at you, *Mammi.*" Again, the Fisher children laughed.

"You cannot argue that it a look of affection," Verity confirmed, grinning at her parents.

"Why have you called us all together like this?" Honor wanted to know. "Surely you could have asked me about this in private."

"No, *liebchen*, this is a family affair. Charity has told us something which I have suspected since you returned here and I want it to be out before all of us so we are clear." Honor waited, her heart thumping furiously.

"You have free will and whatever happens to you is *Gottes Wille*. It is not for us to judge you or turn our backs on you."

"Thank you, *Daed*," Honor whispered, touched that he was again reiterating something he had told her time and again.

He wishes to ensure that I feel loved always. I am so blessed for this family. I will not disappoint them again, certainly not on a fancy I have for some man I barely know.

As if reading her thoughts, Isaac shook his head.

"No, Honor, I need you to listen to me and understand what I am telling you. This applies to everything in your life. I am not speaking of simply entertaining another attraction to an Englisher. I am also speaking of having yourself baptized. That is something you can only do when you are ready, mind, body and soul. It is not something you should do to appease me or anyone else. We love you regardless of what you do but if you chose to be baptized and you are not fully committed, that will be between you and *Gotte*."

Honor gazed at him in horror.

"Daed, I would never stray from the community once I am baptized!" Honor cried passionately but Isaac held up his hand.

"I believe that, Honor. But deceiving yourself and straying from the community are not mutually exclusive ideas. Do you understand?"

It took a long moment for Honor to understand what her father was saying. As the words sunk in, she inhaled deeply.

He is telling me to make sure I know what I want before I commit myself, she thought, her eye shining with gratitude. *He is cautioning me to wait on being baptized until I am certain.*

She choked back her tears and nodded.

"Yes, *Daed,*" she replied, her voice hoarse with emotion. She looked around the room at her family and smiled through her wet, blurry vision.

"Perhaps I will aim for a spring baptism then?" she announced and the room chuckled.

"Oh, Drew!" Charity proclaimed loudly. "How lovely to see you."

"Is Honor here, Charity?" he asked nervously and she nodded, turning to call for her sister but Honor was already coming out through the swinging doors.

"Good morning," Honor chirped, smiling.

"Will you go out on a date with me?" Drew blurted. Charity and Honor exchanged a startled look before Honor turned back to Drew. She ignored her sister as she swallowed a giggle.

"Yes," she replied softly, a sweet smile on her face. "I would like that."

Drew's face melted into a puddle of relief and for the first time since returning home, Honor felt as if she was precisely where she was supposed to be.

THE AMISH GOODBYE

ABIGAIL BAKER

It had taken months of begging and pleading to Mama and Papa, but they finally gave in. Ever since she was a little girl, Abby had an obsession with New York City. There was something about its bustling streets, towering buildings, and even its grit and grime that was so opposite to her small Amish community out in the countryside that unrelentingly called out to her. Each time her family passed through neighboring towns on their way to some market or trade show, she'd soak up every billboard and image depicting the towering skyline of the city that never sleeps.

Abby's parents always thought of her fascination with the city as a passing phase, something all young girls go through in some form or another, but once she turned sixteen she began talking more seriously about leaving home. Mama and Papa went away on rumspringa themselves when they were around her age, but they were still nervous thinking about their only daughter running off to the big city. At first, they insisted she pick a smaller, less intimidating city to visit, like Philadelphia or even Chicago where they had family that could keep on eye on her, but Abby was relentless. They tried to convince her to wait until her younger cousin was old enough to go with her to no avail. Abby had been waiting to go to New York City for as long as she could remember and once she turned eighteen she decided she couldn't wait a single second longer.

That morning, bags packed and dressed for travel, Abby sat down at the breakfast table and told her parents that she was leaving that day, with or without their permission. Not wanting to harbor any ill feelings toward their daughter or to explain to their neighbors that she ran off against their wishes, Mama and Papa gave in with a collective defeated sigh. Abby jumped up like a shot and hugged both her parents at once, almost knocking them to the floor.

"Thank you, thank you, thank you! I promise I'll be okay. Sarah's cousin has an apartment in Manhattan and she said I could stay with her for as long as I want and you don't even have to worry about money because Sarah says everyone in New York serving food at restaurants and it would be super easy for me to get a job, even without any experience or anything. I'll write to you every day, or every other day, or when I have time. It's New York, after all. I'm going to have so much to do! It's all so exciting!"

Abby flashed her parents a bright, enthusiastic smile that they tried to replicate, but their nerves stood in the way. Sarah was Abby's best friend from school. Her parents never let her go on rumspringa because of her cousin, Grace. Grace left home to visit the city when she was eighteen and never came back. Sarah's family was devastated, but Sarah kept in touch with Grace and was assured that she was happy and had made the right choice. Sarah's parents didn't want to take the risk that she might do the same.

"Just...be careful. Remember what you have waiting for you back at home."

"Listen to your Mama. This will always be your home. God has a path set for you here."

Abby brushed off her parents' words of caution with a closed-lipped smile and a small shrug. She understood their concern, but a week, or month, or year in New York wouldn't change her fundamental beliefs, and if it did would that automatically be a bad thing? Grace has lived in New York and away from the church for five years now and she was still a good person. Why did being Amish mean she had to hide herself away from the rest of the world her whole life? If she didn't go see the city she's dreamed of her entire life now then she never would. Besides, she was pretty sure she'd come back home. Her parents shouldn't worry so much.

Mama and Papa insisted she stay for one last meal before she caught the bus one town over that said "New York City" on the front. Abby could barely sit still long enough to bring bites of food to her mouth without shaking them off her fork. She'd seen that bus come and go hundreds of times, but that was the day she'd be going with it. Her mother tried to keep up a normal conversation, but Abby could only respond with "yes" or "no." Her mind was officially elsewhere. Eventually her father excused her from the table and she almost ran right out the door, but a small pang in her stomach stopped her at the threshold. Abby was unquestionably excited to start her journey, but she realized that she would miss her parents along the way. She slowed down for a moment to hug them both goodbye.

"Mama, Papa, I love you both very much. I'll see you when I get back."

She added that last part mostly to reassure her parents, but also a little bit for herself. She'd always imagines what might happen if she decided to stay in New York. She'd work hard to become an actress on Broadway, and one night a handsome fan would come to her dressing room after a particularly stirring performance and confess his love for her. It would turn out that he came from a rich family, of course, and even though she could absolutely support herself being a successful actress and all, she'd be in love and carefree for the rest of her life in a Manhattan penthouse. That was all a harmless fantasy, but the walk to the bus stop was absolutely real. An ounce of nervousness mixed with the excitement swirling around in her head.

She made it just on time, walked on to the half-filled bus, handed her ticket to a stone-faced bus driver and found a seat by the window. She wanted to see every inch of the city as they drove into it. An older woman with a lap full of knitting sat next to her and smiled. The familiarity calmed her a bit. Her mother spent the weekends knitting one and purling two after the morning's chores were finished. It would be a few hours before the skyline even came into view and the slow rocking of the bus soon lulled Abby to sleep.

Two or three hours later, she wasn't sure exactly, a particularly large bump in the road jostled Abby awake. The woman next to her was still knitting what now looked like a child-sized sweater. A quick look out the window revealed the view she'd been dreaming of for eighteen years. Abby clutched the small backpack she brought packed full of all her possessions to her chest and gasped. It was exactly like the pictures, but it also wasn't. Nothing could have prepared her for the jagged line of towering buildings that rose up out of the ground in front of her. The old woman chuckled.

"First time in New York City, dear?"

"Is it that obvious? I've always wanted to visit, but this is the first time my parents actually let me on a bus."

"Well, I prefer the quiet of the country now, but I spent a fair amount of my younger years wandering through the city streets. My daughter lives in Manhattan, so when I visit I get live vicariously through her. I can never stay for too long, though. These old bones can't withstand the hustle and bustle like they used to. Stay out all night for me at least once, will you? There's nothing like Times Square once all the tourists have gone back to their hotels."

Abby tried to assure her that she was going to do everything in New York, especially Times Square, but the woman seemed to lose herself in the memory, smiling down at the knitting in her lap. Abby didn't mind the sudden end to their conversation, it only assured her that sometimes just thinking about being in New York City was better than whatever you were actually doing. Her nails dug into the sides of her backpack as she tried to contain her excitement.

Sarah had given Grace all of Abby's bus information: bus number, time of departure and arrival, where it was going to drop her off. She promised to meet her there and help her figure out the subway.

"I can probably do it on my own. She don't have to go out of her way," Abby had said to Sarah, but Sarah said Grace had laughed kindly and told her there was no way she was going to let an Amish teenage girl get lost in New York on her very first day.

"She might end up wandering around Coney Island and I won't have that."

The streets started to narrow as the bus made it's way deeper into the city and closer to their destination. They passed small corner stores with yellow banners marked "Deli Grocery," and pop-up street vendors selling flowers or fruit or both. Abby tried to remember the face of every new person she saw. Everyone was so different here than in her homogeneous Amish community back home and she loved it. Each unique face had a different story behind it. What did the woman without shoes dressed all in tie-dye do all day? What about the old man in a crisp, tailored suit who read a book while he walked? She loved this city and she hadn't even stepped off the bus yet.

At the bus stop, she recognized Grace right away. Not only could she have been Sarah's somehow older twin, but she was also holding a big poster board sign that said, "Welcome to the Big Apple, Little Amish Girl!" Grace must have recognized her, too, because the moment Abby stepped off the bus she sprinted over and wrapped her in a huge hug, dropping the poster into the street.

"You're finally here! Welcome, welcome, welcome! I'm so excited to have someone from back home come visit me. I love it here, but there's something comfortable about that little town, huh? You excited? You ready for your stay at Casa de Grace?"

Abby knew Grace was kind and outgoing from Sarah's descriptions of her, but she had no idea how energetic she was. Going from the quiet, slow-talking lifestyle back home to Grace's immediate exuberance matched only by the city's chatter behind her was a little overwhelming for her. She could only manage an enthusiastic smile and nod while stumbling over the words, "Yes, okay, I'm ready!" Grace released her from the hug, picked up her sign with one hand, and locked hands with Abby with the other. Abby watched Grace's free-flowing curly hair bounce along behind her as she chatted about everything she wanted to do together while Abby was here. She had dyed it red and let it loose after moving to the city, and Abby admired it. Her dusty blonde locks were almost always pinned tightly to the back of her head and hidden under a bonnet. She left the bonnet at home this time, but the pins remained. She wondered if Grace would help her dye her own hair, maybe black, or blue even. Her parents would love that.

Grace excitedly rattled on about Strawberry Fields in Central Park, and eventually making it to the Statue of Liberty because she hasn't been there in ages, and of course they had to see a Broadway show, there were supposed to be a couple good ones premiering soon, never letting go of Abby's hand. A couple of blocks later, they descended into a subway station and stopped at an automated kiosk to purchase a MetroCard. Abby had never interacted with a machine this complex before and almost froze, not quite knowing what to do with the ball of crumpled bills in her hand. Luckily, Grace was quick to remember what life back home was like and thoughtfully helped her through the process. Holding the bright yellow and blue card in her hand made her feel very grown up and independent. She even made it through the turnstile on the first try.

"You're a natural, Abby! You were made for New York," exclaimed Abby.

Maybe I am, Abby thought.

Mama and Papa may have had more to worry about than a daughter with blue hair.

Grace took a break from listing every attraction in New York City to look down at her cell phone as they took their seats. Abby wrapped her arms tightly around the backpack on her lap and looked around the half-filled car. The subway was a completely new experience for her. She had never been on a bus before, either, but she had seen buses and the types of people on them. *This is like, an underground bus,* she told herself, not completely comfortable with being so far beneath the earth. She focused on the other people sharing the car. Just like the people on the street, no two of them were exactly the same. A tattooed mother sat quietly bouncing a child in her lap, while a teen a few seats down mirrored that image with a boom box blaring hip-hop.

Abby jumped as the train began to move. Grace chuckled and put a hand on her arm.

"I did the same thing on my first subway ride. Turned out I was on the right train but headed the wrong way so I had bigger fish to fry than dealing with being on a train for the first time," she threw back her head and laughed at the memory. "Once I realized I was no where near where I wanted to be I got off the train and started asking people which train would take me where I needed to be and they just kept telling me the one I was on. I didn't realize that the train going in the right direction was just on the other side of the platform. Man, did I feel dumb, but you won't have to worry about that, you have me!"

The two girls chatted for a little while as the train made it's way to their stop. Once they emerged back onto the city streets Abby began to get a feel for the constant flow of people. She quickened her pace to match Grace's and only bumped shoulders with a handful of people as she weaved through the crowd. Eventually, they walked into a tall building where a man sat at a desk by the door.

"Morning, Fred! This is my, well, she's basically my cousin. Abby's gonna be staying with me for a while so don't surprised if she comes flying through here at all hours of the day, okay?"

"Not a problem, Gracie! A friend of yours is a friend of mine. Nice to meet you, Abby!"

Abby smiled and waved at him as they walked to the elevator. She was surprised at how friendly everyone seemed to be. On the odd occasion that she did get her parents to talk with her about New York all they had to say about it was how unwholesome and rude the people were. She'd have to tell them how wrong they were when she got back. *If* she went back.

"That's my doorman, Fred. He's awesome. Always happy to see you even in the middle of the night. If you get yourself locked out or something and I'm not around Fred will help you out."

"That's good to know, thanks. Is everyone in New York this friendly?"

Grace laughed again.

"Not at all. Don't get me wrong, you'll find friendly people if you look for them but a lot of people would run you over with their cars and never look back. They're not bad people, they just have things to do and places to be and no time to stop and check if you're alive or not. That's your problem."

Grace saw a look of dismay cross over Abby's face.

"Don't worry, though. I'll make sure to introduce you to all the best people in New York. You just make sure not to get hit by any cars."

The elevator dinged as they made it to the fourteenth floor. Grace's apartment was at the end of the hall. It had two bedrooms, both with views overlooking the busy streets below, a small kitchen, a bathroom to share, and a living room filled with paintings and posters and a million other colorful decorations. Abby noticed a picture of Grace and Sarah from years ago sitting on a table by the couch. Before she could walk over to get a better look, Grace waved her into one of the two bedrooms. The room had a few pieces of art on the walls, but wasn't near as covered as the living room. A small bed was pushed up against the wall and dresser sat across from it with a TV placed on top.

"This is your room! I moved a bunch of stuff out of it and into the living room so you wouldn't be overwhelmed. I've only been here for a couple of years but I've managed to collect so much junk. I guess that's what happens when you go from a simple Amish life on the family farm to the big city. I can show you how to use the TV, too. I wouldn't blame you if you spent your first couple of days here just sitting in front of it watching cartoons. I know I did."

It was tempting, but Abby had been waiting to be a part of this city for so long she almost felt cooped up just being in the room to drop her things off.

"I'll definitely watch some TV later, but right now all I want is to explore or maybe find I job. I promised my parents I wouldn't ask them for money."

"Oh! I forgot to tell you. I know the manager of the diner down the street. He said he was looking for waitresses so I told him about you. He wants you to come down tomorrow morning so he can make sure you're not a total klutz or anything but you've basically got the job! How do you feel about pancakes?"

"I love pancakes! Thank you so much, Grace. You've done too much already."

"Don't even worry about it. I know what it's like being cooped up on a farm with no electricity or entertainment or fun. I want to make sure you're trip is the complete opposite of that! All fun, all the time. So, what do you want to do first?"

They spent the rest of the day just walking around Manhattan. They stopped for coffee at a sidewalk café, bought a few outfits fit for work at a department store, watched the dogs run around at the dog park. It was a fairly average day in New York but to Abby it was the best day of her life. Grace was a wealth of information, only stopping the flow to take sips of her latte. She knew the best place to get a burger, the best place for live music, the best cup of coffee – this wasn't it, but it would do.

"It's almost dinner time so why don't we start with the best Chinese takeout and spend the evening just hanging out at my place. How does that sound? You must be exhausted!"

She was exhausted, but she'd never admit it. She could only agree that Chinese food did sound good, even though she'd never had it before, and she wouldn't mind a night in. They stopped at a hole-in-the-wall restaurant only distinguishable by its vaguely oriental décor. Grace never once looked at the menu as she rattled off a list of food: crab rangoons, fried rice, sweet and sour chicken, lo mien, and don't forget the fortune cookies! When they got back to the apartment, Grace spread the feast out on her coffee table, handed Abby a pair of chopsticks, and said "Dig in!" After some fumbling with the sticks, she was able to shovel mountains of delicious and greasy food into your mouth.

While they watched the movie "Mean Girls," one of Grace's favorites, Abby broke open a fortune cookie. One side listed a handful of lucky numbers and the other said, "A big surprise is coming your way." She had spent so much time planning for this trip, accounting for every little detail, she wondered what surprises the city could possibly have in store for her. She could hardly sleep that night thinking about it. Maybe she wouldn't get the job. Maybe New York wouldn't live up to her expectations, but that couldn't be it because they already had. Maybe it would be something else, something so surprising that she couldn't even imagine it yet. She hoped that was it.

***

In the morning, Grace woke Abby up with a gentle shake and a steaming cup of coffee.

"Morning sunshine! It's your first day of work and I don't want you to be late. Here, I made you some coffee and I picked out an outfit for you last night, but you don't have to wear it. Sorry I'm acting like such a mom after you came all this way to get away from your parents. Yikes!"

Abby laughed, "I wasn't running *away* from my parents, I was running *to* New York! Thank you for the pleasant wakeup call."

"Well, I was definitely running from my parents. Living in that house was stifling; all those rules, no fun, and for what? God's plan? Sorry, I just get a little frustrated sometimes thinking about all the things my parents kept from me back home. I still feel religious from time to time, but the rigid rules of Amish life just aren't for me."

"Yeah, I know what you mean. I feel like there's so much I want to do that I just can't there. That's why I wanted to come here. I want to get it all out of my system so that I can go back to living simply. Once I've done everything I'll probably be so exhausted that I'll want to go back anyways!"

Grace smiled at her kindly, but bit her tongue. She knew better than most that it didn't always work that way. She didn't want to influence Abby's choice either way, but life as she saw it couldn't just be flushed out of someone's system. A person either craves an Amish life, or an English one. Abby just had to decide which it was she wanted most.

"We can talk about the serious stuff later. Why don't you jump in the shower and get ready for work while I cook breakfast. Go ahead and use whatever you find in there. Mi shampoo es tu shampoo!"

Abby washed herself, changed into the clothes Grace picked out for her, and played around with her makeup. Back home she didn't have any of this stuff. You didn't need makeup to go to church. Plus, every boy she knew had known her since they were children. They'd just be confused if she showed up to the Sunday sing one day covered in powders and creams, but here, no one knew her. She could wear as much or as little makeup as she wanted and no one would question it. Abby decided to start small, only applying a small amount of blush and a couple coats of mascara. The thick frame of lashes made her eyes look huge and the soft pink on her cheeks gave her the appearance of being a little bit warm. Even this small amount of makeup looked jarring in the mirror, but she also kind of liked it.

When she finally emerged from the bathroom Grace was dancing around her kitchen using a spatula as a microphone. At the end of an exaggerated spin she saw Abby standing in the hall giggling.

"Hey! You look awesome! You even threw on some makeup? That's advance level stuff. Now you just need to learn to flirt a little bit and you'll be swimming in tips."

"I know how to flirt!" Abby said defensively.

"Ha! Staring at a boy across the room during prayer is not flirting. New York's a completely different world."

"Oh yeah? How different can city boys be?"

"You know what? You might be right. All you have to do is blink those big doe eyes at one of these too-cool-for-school guys and they'll be smitten. You'll do fine."

"I don't even know if I want to date anyways."

"Oh, you'll change your mind the first time a cute boy tells you he likes your smile. Trust me. It happens to the best of us."

They talked a little bit about boys and back home over breakfast before it was time for Abby to head to the diner. It was so close to Grace's apartment building that she brought Abby down to the lobby, pointed to the place on the corner, sent her on her way and told her to ask for a man named Greg. She was a little nervous to go on her own, but this was exactly the experience that she was hoping to have in New York. Abby craved a taste of independence and she was finally getting it.

The diner was called "Rizzo's Place" and it looked exactly how she'd pictured a classic New York diner. The tables and chairs were all covered in turquoise vinyl complete with little flecks of glitter and the wait staff were all wearing crisp white aprons and matching paper hats. The aprons reminded her of her mother's back home, but that was the only ounce of familiarity she felt. The restaurant was fairly busy. Early morning was their rush hour, but that had passed so only a handful of stragglers and early lunch-eaters remained. She was standing by the doorway when a man only a little older than her wandered over to see if she wanted a table.

"Hey there! Can I help you?"

"I'm looking for Greg. I'm supposed to start working today."

The man's face broke out into a huge smile and he leaned in for a hug.

"You must be Abby! Grace told me all about you and how hardworking and great you are. Grace and I are like this," he crossed his fingers to show that they were close, "so I'd do anything for that girl. Oh! I'm Greg by the way."

Abby gathered from his tone that he might be gay. She had met one gay boy before back in her town, but he hadn't told anyone aside from her and a few friends about his sexuality. It wasn't something that bothered her, but seeing a man so openly flamboyant surprised and encouraged her. She had always thought of New York as a place where everyone could be exactly who they wanted to be, and seeing this man live up to that ideal was exciting. Abby smiled back and nodded.

"That's me! Thank you so much for giving me this job."

"You're so cute! Abby, you're going to fit in just fine here. I almost don't even think I have to train you. Want to just throw on an apron and dive right in?"

When a nervous look crossed over Abby's face he added, "All you have to do first is introduce yourself and ask if they'd like anything to drink. They usually just want coffee or water. If they want coffee make sure to ask about cream and sugar. I'll only give you one table for now so don't worry! If you flop, I'll be here to help you out but you seem like a natural!"

Greg scoped the restaurant to see which table he wanted to throw at her.

"Okay, there's one guy sitting in the corner. He's a regular. He usually just comes in for a coffee, sometimes scrambled eggs with a side of bacon, but nothing too complicated. Nice guy. Are you ready?"

Abby nodded. Greg smiled and gently pushed her forward. She didn't realize how quickly she'd be thrown into the actual serving part of the job, but she wasn't about to embarrass herself so she threw back her shoulders and approached the table as confidently as she could.

"Hey there! I'm Abby. Can I get you a coffee to drink? I mean, can I get you anything?"

From far away she couldn't tell how subtly attractive the man in the booth was. He was partially hidden by a beanie hat and an oversize sweatshirt, but when she got closer Abby could see a sharp jaw line and kind eyes beneath the baggy outerwear. She was thrown off by her attraction for a moment, but her desire to impress her new boss prevailed. She flashed him a professional smile as she bit her tongue.

"Yeah, sure, a black coffee would be great."

"Can I get you anything else?"

"Not right now, thanks."

She turned on her heal and walked back to Greg, not sure where she was supposed to take the order. Luckily, he was watching enthusiastically from the sidelines cheering her on silently.

"How'd it go? Was he nice? What am I saying, he's always nice! What did he order?'"

"Just a black coffee."

"Yep, that sounds like him. Let me show you where the coffee station is."

Greg helped her find the station and pour a cup. He showed her where the cream and sugar was, just in case her next customer needed it. He then showed her how to use the computer system in order to keep track of what each customer ordered. This was all very simple, however, and it wasn't long until she was right back at her only customer's table with the cup of coffee.

"Here you are, sir. One cup of black coffee."

"Thanks, but why are you talking like that. It sounds like you're a robot who was programmed to work in a diner."

Abby blushed.

"Oh, well it's my first day. Sorry. I'm still trying to get the hang of things."

The customer looked a little embarrassed as well. He didn't mean to call her out.

"No, I mean, I'm sorry. I didn't mean to embarrass you. Thanks for the coffee. It's great, as always."

Abby gave him a polite, but uncomfortable, half smile and turned to walk away but he stopped her.

"Wait, what's your name?"

"Abby."

"Abby, like Abigail?"

"No. Just Abby, actually. My mom just liked Abby."

"That's a nice name. Mine's Mac, like Mackenzie. My mom wanted a girl, but got me instead, so she picked a gender-neutral name. I don't mind it, though."

"I like Mac. There aren't a lot of guys where I'm from with names like that."

"Oh yeah? Where is it that you're from?"

"It's a little Amish town just outside of here, actually. I just got into the city yesterday."

"Yesterday? You need someone to show you around then."

Abby blushed again. She thought about what Grace said about flirting for tips, but this felt more genuine than that. This guy, Mac, didn't seem to care about tips.

"I'd like that."

"Great! Give me your phone number and I'll call you up sometime."

"Oh, I don't have a phone number. I don't have a phone."

"That's right. The whole 'Amish' thing. Well, when do you get off here?"

Greg had been listening in the whole time and jumped into the conversation.

"Right now! She's done for the day, wasn't she amazing? I just have to teach her how to clock out and she'll be on her way!"

Greg pulled Abby to the side to chat, but Abby was confused.

"Did I do something wrong? Do you not want me to work here?"

"No! No, of course not. I've just seen this guy come in day in, day out and, don't get me wrong he's one of the nicest customers we have which is why I'm doing this, but he's never once brought in a date or left with one. It's just so cute seeing you two together I can't resist! Go! Have a good time and come back tomorrow and we'll give you some real training. It was my mistake for giving you the cute, single guy as your first table."

Abby almost didn't know what to do. She expected to start her first job, but instead she was going on her first date. She walked back over to Mac's table, Greg casually waving his hands to encourage her.

"Sorry about that. It looks like I'm free now."

"Great! I can take you to work with me then."

Abby had no idea what this entailed but Greg gave her a thumbs up and she followed Mac out of the diner. They walked for a few blocks, casually chatting about their lives. Mac was very interested in Abby's Amish community and Abby was very interested in where Mac was taking her. If it hadn't been for Greg's insistence, she probably wouldn't have felt comfortable following a man she just met through New York City, but she couldn't resist. Eventually, he led them into a building and up a few flights of stairs. Greg pulled back a sliding iron door to reveal a colorful studio filled with paintings and sculptures.

"This is where I work, and live, I guess."

"You're an artist!" Abby exclaimed.

"I'd like to think so, but I've been in a rut lately. I haven't been able to create anything new. I don't want to sound cliché, but would you mind if I tried painting you? You haven't even taken off your work apron yet and your eyes are just so beautiful."

He didn't comment on her smile, but Grace's words still ran through her mind as this boy asked if she'd model for him. On one hand, she was weary, but on the other his sincerity penetrated through most else. She didn't feel as though he wanted anything from her except for her image so she agreed. Mac and Abby sat mostly still for the next couple of hours as Mac swept acrylics across a large canvas, capturing Abby in that moment. When the painting was finally done he turned it around and approached her.

"Alright, here it is. How do you like it?"

Abby looked at herself, carefully depicted in paint. Mac had noticed her mascara covered eyes, but hadn't painted them in a cartoonish way. He'd only enhanced the features on her face that had already been beautiful.

"It's...gorgeous! Is that conceded to say?"

"No, not when you look like you do."

Mac leaned towards Abby to kiss her. She almost turned away, but her instincts took over. With his mouth on hers she finally felt free of her parents grasp and also just free in general. He pulled away before she was finished enjoying the moment.

"I don't want to overstep my boundaries here. I like you a lot, but where from two different worlds."

Abby smiled confidently for the first time and touched his face.

"This is exactly what I want," she said before leaning back in to finish the kiss.

***

The two teens dated for a few weeks after that first studio session. Abby posed for multiple paintings, some more revealing than others, but always with her expressed consent. She loved having her freedom. She loved being able to come and go from Grace's apartment as she wished, but eventually she got bored. One night, as Mac painted Abby holding a bouquet of roses while sitting on a couch, she finally hit her breaking point. She threw the roses up into the air and started to shout.

"Mac! I can't do this anymore. What's the point of me coming here, day after day, just to be your model?"

"You're gorgeous, Abby. You're my muse!"

"But what am I getting out of this? Where does this take me?"

Mac couldn't answer that and Abby got up to leave.

"This has been fun, Mac, but I don't have a purpose here. I think I need to go home."

Mac tried to convince her to stay. He tried to convince her that her portraits meant more to him than just simple trinkets, but she wasn't swayed. As fun as the city was, as much freedom as she had, home would always be back in her little farm town. God had always had a path laid out for her, and this turned out to be only a detour.

LOVINA

ELAINE STEPHENS

Lovina rolled over in her cotton sheets and stared out the window at the sun beaming through the ragged curtains of her bedroom. The light from the morning lit up the interior of her modest room. The cock crowed as she stirred and stepped from the comfort of the warm bed. As her delicate toes touched the floor she winced at the feel of the cool floorboards beneath her feet. She mentally prepared herself for another typical day in the remote Amish community where she was raised. She sat on the edge of her bed and began braiding her long, golden locks. Her hair had never been cut. Once finished she tied a tiny, white bow at the end. Standing up, her hair extended all the way down to her upper thighs.

From the homely bedside table, she grabbed her prayer cap, the white cap made of organza and stiff with starch that she must wear in public. She slipped it over her long, golden braid and stood, making her way over to the wardrobe, barefoot. The floorboards creaked beneath her slender frame. The house in which she lived was in need of much repair, but it was home.

Her dress was bound by the Amish community to which she belonged. She pulled out the calf-length, gray dress, and her white apron to accompany it. She looked the outfit up and down, sighing at the restrictions she had to abide by. Just a little color or a little lace would make it so much more tolerable, but alas it was forbidden.

She slipped the dress over her head, atop the white, cotton undergarments she wore beneath. Her slender arms penetrated the long sleeves at the ends and her delicate fingers stretched out toward the floor. Her blue eyes reflected in the full-length mirror that stood opposite. They ran over her entire frame, assessing the modesty of her attire. Her smooth legs peeked out the bottom of the gown. Her hands just protruded from the sleeves. How she longed for something different. To have somewhat more choice when it came to the little things. But living here her options were overly restricted. With a sigh, she turned away from her dull reflection.

Her stomach growled lightly, alerting her that breakfast time was upon her. Before leaving, she quickly raced to the window and opened it wide, allowing the cool morning air to hit her face. It almost stung as the contrasting wind nipped at her warm skin. She turned on her heels and made her way to the exit of her humble sanctuary, ready to start the day ahead.

Before opening the door she took a deep breath, hearing the faint clip-clop of hooves outside. She felt a tear well up in the corner of her eye, but she willed it to stop. No matter how much she tried, Lovina was overwhelmed with pain with any reminder of her parent's accident. No day since their passing had her parent's death become any easier for Lovina. Each day she was reminded of the terrible accident they had undertaken. As soon as she set eyes on the cart outside, laying rusted and disheveled. Unused for a year. A constant visual scar, sitting in their front yard. Although she knew that her brother, Jacob, shared her pain she would not dare discuss with him.

He had been walking down the street when it occurred. On his way back from the cornfields down the road from their home. Their mother and father waved as they passed, smiling at him. The next thing Jacob knew, he was watching their cart overturn as the horses bucked and bolted, leaving the two bodies trapped beneath the wreckage. Around him, people screamed at the sight, but all he could do was rush over to find his parents laying lifeless in the middle of the dirt road.

Lovina was distraught. She cried for weeks. She took to her room and moped. No one could comfort her. Since then the community had done their best to assist the two orphaned children. They stayed in the family home, but here they could barely make ends meet. Her job as a milkmaid at the dairy farm and his as an apprentice blacksmith left them living pay day to pay day. They relied on handouts from neighbors and friends to feed themselves. Still, Lovina and Jacob vowed to take care of themselves, and that was just what they did. Regardless of if it was against the rules.

One evening, months after the accident, Jacob had an idea. He weighed it up in his mind over and over. He had promised Lovina the day of their parents passing that he would always take care of her. That was just what he intended to do. But not if it meant risking her safety or standing within the community. Finally, he decided that there was no other option for them. The need for financial stability was too great.

"Come out with me tonight," he had asked, his voice trembling with what she felt to be nerves, excitement or worry, she could not distinguish.

"To where?" she had asked, but he would not answer. Lovina was wary at first of her brother's sudden plan. Still, she trusted him and so she followed, through the woods and to the city on the other side.

"Where are we going, Jacob?" she asked on their journey. He turned and held out his hand, signaling her to stop in her tracks. He opened the knapsack he had been holding tightly to his chest since they had left the community. Inside was a range of colorful clothing, the likes of which Lovina had never seen.

"I am taking you to the city," he explained, pulling out a pale pink fitted dress and white heels for his sister. She stared in awe at the strange fabric garments handed to her.

"You need to wear these, otherwise they will know we are not from there," he explained. Entering a modern city in their modest attire would surely give them away as patrons of the well-known Amish district just miles away. Jacob had experienced this prejudice first hand after all.

"I will stand over there. Let me know when you have changed. You can put your clothes in this bag," he gestured to the bag from which he had pulled the new outfit. Then he turned and walked out of sight, giving his sister the privacy to change.

She untied her apron and dropped her dress to the forest floor. She folded them and placed them in the knapsack Jacob had provided. She shivered in the cold night air. Picking up the new dress she pulled it gingerly over her head. It was so tight and firm around her body. She looked down at herself in the odd creation. Quickly she slipped the heels on her feet and called out,

"I think I am ready Jacob!" moments later he emerged from the shadows. He paused, taken aback by his sister's speedy transformation. He took her hand and kicked the knapsack into a large bush beside them.

"Time to go then," he whispered and they were off again through the trees.

When they came out on the other side of the vast wood, Lovina stopped in awe. The lights glistened in the distance as they looked over the high-rise jungle. Jacob had been lucky enough to experience life on the other side. This is where he had been during Rumspringa, but his freedom was short-lived. He promptly returned to the community, overwhelmed by the progression he experienced.

Lovina had not had that luxury. This was her first time in the city, even seeing it from a distance.

"Why are you bringing me here?" she mumbled. Jacob's expression became serious.

"We need money, Lovina. I did not want to worry you with such matters but since our parents passing we have been struggling... more than you know." she had no idea what this had to do with going to the city.

"We can get jobs here. Second jobs, at night. It has been so hard for us Annaliese and I need your help. Please," he begged. But she would do anything for her brother. She took his hand once more and squeezed it kindly.

"Then let's go," she said, excitedly.

Months later and they had been working at the diner quite regularly, almost every night. Lovina darted around in her short, yellow waitressing uniform, serving tables left and right. After her first day, she was amazed at how much money she had made, and just in tips. In the kitchen her brother worked hastily, cleaning dish after dish and piles of cutlery. But neither of them minded the hard work, especially Lovina. She was happy to just be out in the real world.

"Order up!" the chef boomed from the service window. He rang the bell relentlessly to alert her of food being ready to pick up. She scooted over and took it to her waiting customers. Now she had everything down to a fine art.

The sneaking around was getting quite cumbersome, however. Her heart raced each night her and Jacob ventured out, against the communities wishes. That night when she got home she collapsed on the bed and stared up at the ceiling. Exhausted, she wished her life was more simple. Leading her dual existence was taking its toll on her. She was plagued with a lack of sleep and a crippling anxiety. Tossing and turning during her few hours sleep each night. Alas, she had no other choice, for now anyway. She felt a huge debt weighing on her, for her brother. He had taken care of Lovina since their parent's sudden demise. No matter how much she wished she could leave, it was not an option.

One morning as she was walking down the street, Lovina was greeted by an unexpected face.

"Lovina!" a man's voice boomed from behind her. She turned quickly on her heel to see an old friend, one whom she thought had left for good years earlier.

"Jebidiah?" she said, stunned. Her grocery basket fell to the ground with a thud as she ran toward him and wrapped her arms around his broad shoulders. He picked her up around the waist and they held their embrace for several seconds. Even though it had been so long since their last encounter, neither failed to recognize the other.

He dropped her back to the ground and she stepped back slightly to take in the sight of her long lost friend. His hair was styled just as it always had been. His dark brown locks were cut short, a few inches from his scalp. It hung in waves around his face. His skin was tanned and contrasted perfectly with his strong, masculine jawline and muscular figure. His chin was littered with stubble, giving his face a slight shadowing.

Their last meeting had not been so joyous. Jebidiah had been leaving for Rumspringa with her brother Jacob. The three children had grown up as close as they could be, spending endless hours together playing in the cornfields and chasing each other through the streets. Since the age of five, Lovina and Jebidiah had known each other. She saw him as one of her closest friends. Or at least she had before he disappeared.

It had been a cold night, pelting down with rain. They stood there, facing each other. Lovina had been fifteen, Jebidiah sixteen. Not a word was spoken for several minutes between them. Too young to realize the deep feelings that connected them, Jebidiah left with Jacob, to experience the modern world with the rest of the community boys coming of age that year. Lovina had waited for him. She waited up at night and watched for him during the day. But he did not return.

Jacob came back weeks later with a few of the neighborhood boys, but Jebidiah was not among them.

Her brother had rested his hand on her shoulder as tears rolled down her face, tears for the loss of her best friend.

"He said to tell you he will see you again. He promised." at the time Lovina had not believed him. She had thought her brother was trying desperately to bring her out of her deepening hole of overwhelming sadness. But with Jebidiah standing before her, Jacob's words echoed in the midst of her thoughts.

'He promised.'

She had given up hope of seeing him again, yet here he stood, in the flesh.

Jebidiah was speechless. He had returned to the community after years. It seemed that no matter how much the modern world drew him, his love for Lovina was stronger. From the day he had left, he did not stop thinking about her, not for a moment. It had been fun and he savored the new experiences put forth by his peers in the city, but no one could replace her. That was what influenced him to return. There was nothing more he could gain from the city, he was looking to start a family. Jebidiah could not consider anyone else he would rather make a life with than her.

"I hope Jacob gave you my message all those years ago," he said, smiling down at her from above.

"He did," she replied, mirroring the beam that had taken over Jebidiah's face. Any onlooker could tell that these two were much more than just friends, even if they had not yet admitted it to themselves. They still grasped the hands of each other as they chatted for a few minutes about shared memories from the past.

Jebidiah bent down and picked up the discarded basket of groceries Lovina had dropped in her shock at his appearance.

"Let's go for a walk, I need to catch up with you. So much has happened in the last few years I am sure," he laughed. As they strolled along they spoke at length about their experiences. Everything Jebidiah said about his time away absolutely intrigued her. She desperately wished that she could share in this modern world, if only for a day. Working was all she had ever had the chance to do when her and Jacob managed to escape for their night shifts.

"So, what about your life, Lovina?" he questioned. After a moment of thought, he saw her face drop. The only significant thing she could think of to tell him was of her parent's sudden demise the previous fall. She took a deep breath and prepared herself for the retelling of the most painful memory she possessed.

"Actually, there was an accident last year," she began. Jebidiah's permanent grin faded almost immediately.

"My parents cart overturned. It was terrifying but the worst was that they did not make it." Jebidiah could not find the words to express his condolences. After a few moments to comprehend the brief and saddening story he mustered,

"I am so sorry, Lovina."

As always, her first thought was to change the subject, and so she did. Long ago she had decided that her parents would not have wanted her to mourn, but cherish the life that she had. That was exactly what she intended to do. The sadness they had been wallowing in for that brief moment evaporated quickly as they moved on to more trivial and light-hearted news from their vast time apart.

Jebidiah walked her all the way back to her door. He handed back the basket as she stepped through the threshold of the dark, polished doorway.

"Well, I am sure we will see each other again soon," he said as he turned to leave.

"You will," she smiled and with that the door clicked shut behind her.

As the following months flew by, Lovina found herself spending more and more of her limited free time with her long lost friend. Jebidiah found comfort in their closeness. Since moving back, he had faced endless scrutiny from the older members of the place he called home. They frowned upon him for his rash decision to leave, now that he had returned. He had known upon his abrupt return to his family that not everyone would be so welcoming. But no one else mattered as long as Lovina was by his side.

She found comfort in his company too. She was intrigued by his endless stories of the new technologies and strange architecture he had encountered in his years away. Unlike her peers, Lovina held nothing against him for leaving, if anything she wished that she could do the same.

The two companions spent their time just as they did, years earlier. Exploring the now familiar woods. Chasing each other through the cornfields. Collapsing with laughter on the dirt floor of the outdoors.

They savored each moment they spent in each others company. To Lovina, no one could compare to Jebidiah.

One sunny afternoon, they fell into each other's arms in the dewy grass of the outskirts of the boundary. Their laughter subsided and Lovina looked up at Jebidiah, beaming down at her. She knew that there was something deeper. This was not just another friendship, he meant so much more. Every second without him left her feeling cold and empty. Every second without her made him feel as if he was completely alone.

"Do you think you will stay here this time?" Lovina asked. She hoped that his answer reflected the way that she felt. But alas, he uttered the answer she did not want to hear.

"No. I think that now I have experienced what is out there, lived my life outside the confines of the community, I don't want to leave again." her heart dropped. There was nothing in the world she wished for more than to go, but a life without Jebidiah seemed just as empty.

It was his strength that encouraged her to plan her escape, to a new life in the modern world. Deep in her heart she knew that it was unlikely Jebidiah would come with her. After all, he had returned not weeks ago, but she had to follow her dreams. She had but one life, and she intended to live it. As much as she wanted to share with him her wishes, she knew this was one secret she must keep to herself.

Jebidiah walked her home again that day, as he often did of late. The sun was setting over the sovereign hills as they strolled past people and places on the way home. She took in the sights, for in a few weeks they would be gone forever. There was no doubt she would miss this place, but most of all she would miss him. She cherished the time they had together, though short lived.

They arrived at her home. Before she opened the door, Jebidiah grasped her wrist tightly. Her skin broke out in goosebumps all over in response to his flesh against hers. Her heart raced within her chest cavity. Cheeks began to glow red as the blood from her pounding heart rushed to her face. She hoped that Jebidiah did not see the intense reaction she gave from his touch.

"Do you have plans for tomorrow?" he questioned. His expression was serious all of a sudden.

"No," Lovina responded. Where was he going with this?

"I see, well goodnight then," he said with a grin. How strange. With that Jebidiah let go of her arm and placed his hands into his pockets.

"Goodbye," she called to him as he strolled slowly away, toward his family home at the end of the road.

As she closed the door behind her Lovina leaned her back against the rough wood and closed her eyes. The overwhelming sensation of lust she felt for Jebidiah was quickly blooming into a raging passion. Love. Little did she know that he felt it too. From the top of her head to the far tips of her toes her entire being was filled with admiration and desire for him. How would she tell him that she was going to leave the town? Start a new life in the place that he had run from.

She already had a plan in place. Two weeks from now she would be living amongst the modern world. Jacob had not been pleased, but he knew that he could not stop his sister from following her dreams. He had the opportunity, so there was no way that he could deny her that right, regardless of the community law.

"Are you sure you will be OK on your own?" Jacob could not hide the worried tone of his voice. Not even he could brave the new world, how could his little sister live there alone?

"I will, please do not worry about me, Jacob," then she explained her plan.

In the dead of night, while the town slept, she would sneak silently through the streets. Toward the wood. The path that they had traveled hundreds of times before would lead her to her new existence. She could not leave during the day, for fear of what scrutiny she may face from the others in the town. Women rarely left and were never welcomed home. It was best for her to just disappear.

"But you have never been that way alone." he said, his voice still trembling with fear for Lovina.

"I have mapped out our way. The last few weeks I have made a note of each landmark along the path. Each time I feel as if my feet lead me more and more. I step without hesitation." slowly she had memorized the way. Every rock and tree, branch and shrub. The dirt clearings and the overgrown mangling of tangled weeds, she was confident in her navigational ability. Even if Jacob was not so.

"Where will you stay?" his questions kept coming. But Lovina was not one to take her decisions lightly. To his every question, she had the perfect answer. During their time at the diner, they had made a few friends, both co-workers, and customers. Lovina had organized a room in a modest apartment with Katie, a fellow waitress at a neighboring restaurant. For only a small portion of her minimum wage, she had a place to her her own.

Several hours later, Lovina had assured her brother that she could fend for herself. If she ever needed him, he would be there for her too.

Jacob took her hand and looked at her, eyes full of sadness.

"I will always be here for you, sister," a single tear rolled down his cheek, winding its way through the stubble on his strong chin. Lovina was taken aback, she had not seen her brother so emotional since their parents passing. She whispered the only words that came to mind in response to his heartfelt confession.

"I know," tears now flowed freely down their faces. They sat in silence as Jacob took in the news she had revealed to him. The plan she had derived. How much he would miss her.

The hardest part was over. Lovina had dreaded telling her brother about her escape. Now she felt free, with his blessing she could leave without hesitation. She slept that night, soundly for the first time in many moons. Dreaming of the future adventures she would have in the big city.

The next morning Jebidiah was at her door before either of the siblings had risen. She heard the light tapping from her bedroom and quickly dressed to see who was so desperate to see them this day. She raced down the creaking steps and to the front door. Opening it widely she was ecstatic to see Jebidiah standing there with a bouquet of red roses. Their scent was swept immediately into her nostrils and she closed her eyes as the aroma intoxicated her.

"Good morning, Lovina," Jebidiah greeted her, placing the stunning bunch into her hands.

"Hello," she replied, staring at the gift he had brought for her. Something was different about him this morning. She could not pick it but his smile was strange somehow, brighter than she had seen before. His eyes sparkled in the morning light. Her heart skipped a beat as they paused for a moment, looking deeply into each other's eyes.

"I have a day planned for us," he said excitedly. Before she had time to properly lace up her boots, Jebidiah took her hand and whisked her away from her home. They walked together toward the vast cornfields at the end of the street. Waving at their fellow community members as they passed, Jebidiah led Lovina through the tall corn stalks.

She had no idea what he had in store. They rushed forward in silence. Lovina found her mind wandering as she took in the rays of sunlight winding through the stalks and leaves surrounding them. Her dress occasionally caught on rouge sticks and branches strewn throughout the fields. She stumbled a few times, but Jebidiah was there to catch her and help her find her feet once more.

Minutes passed and they finally arrived at the small clearing in the far end of the fields. Jebidiah let her hand drop and pulled a blanket from the backpack he had been lugging with them on the short journey. He laid it delicately out on the ground, straightening the edges and patting it down flat.

"Come, sit," he gestured to a soft spot on the blanket and she slowly approached, sitting down carefully, holding her dress flat against her thighs as she lowered her body to the ground. She watched on as Jebidiah began unpacking a picnic that he had prepared. She was stunned at the romantic setting that he had created for just the two of them, out of nowhere.

"I hope you're hungry," he laughed. Her eyes drifted from plate to plate, each piled high with sandwiches and cakes, fruit and salads. She could not believe what she saw before her. This was the kind of thing she had always dreamed of but had never eventuated into a reality. The sun beamed down on them as they began their conversations.

"Please," Jebidiah picked up a plate of her favorite sandwiches, fresh strawberry jam. She picked up one and took a bite. The sweetness of the jam found every corner of her tongue, leaving a lasting sensation in her mouth as she swallowed. He watched her intently, looking as if something was weighing heavily on his mind. Lovina looked into his deep, brown eyes. She felt herself smile as she took in his handsome features, just inches from her. His short, dark hair flowed subtly in the mild breeze. Her gaze followed his masculine jawline and rugged chin, covered in light stubble.

It was at that moment Jebidiah uttered the words she had been longing for him to say for so long,

"I love you, Lovina, I always have." she was taken aback. Of course, her heart reciprocated his feelings, but she could not bring herself to say the words back. In the back of her mind, she knew that if she revealed her love for him she must also let him in on the fact she was planning to leave. Leave him and everything else behind. Moments later she found her voice once more,

"I love you too."

They spoke for hours after Jebidiah's unexpected, but heartfelt, confession. Of life and the paths they wanted to take in the future. That was when troubles arose.

"I just want to settle down, and have a family. I love it so much here. It feels so right to be back." Jebidiah said in between bites of his rosy red apple. Lovina froze. This was exactly the life she was running from. It was the first time that she realized that their journeys may lead them in different directions. She sat silent for a moment as he waited patiently for her to say something, anything. She took a deep breath and proceeded to reveal her underlying plan to Jebidiah. Her plan to leave and start a new life in the city he had fled from.

"I had no idea," Jebidiah gasped, in response to her and Jacob's secret second existence outside of the community. His heart dropped as she continued to explain her plans to escape and live amongst the modern world. Never had he thought coming into the fields with her that morning that she would drop this bombshell upon him. All hopes of his quiet life back at home with his childhood sweetheart were slowly evaporating before his eyes.

"When do you plan to leave?" he questioned, his heartbeat pounding in his chest. He prayed that it was not soon. That he would have time to change her mind.

"Two weeks from today," she admitted. His smile had faded, and hers with it. She had thought that the hardest conversation before her departure was over, but she had not counted on Jebidiah's romantic notions. His proposal of a simple, family life in the mundane town she had always lived. She loved him deeply, but her want for adventure was overwhelming.

With the sun beginning to lower over the tips of the corn, they decided that it was time to return. She folded the blanket as Jebidiah picked up the empty plates that surrounded them in the clearing. He took her hand and led the way back through the towering stalks. They moved at a much slower pace upon their return. Lovina could not be sure, maybe it was due to the dimming light, but she felt as if their lagging pace was a bi-product of the conversations they had just had. Of her leaving him and the rest of her life behind.

Eventually, they reached her front door once more. She stepped up the front stair and peered down at him.

"Thank you for today, Jebidiah. I had an amazing time. I really appreciate all that you have done for me," Lovina checked quickly for onlookers and before a word could escape his lips she kissed him tenderly on the cheek. By the time Jebidiah realized what had happened she had already stepped back inside.

He began his journey home, filled with mixed emotions from the day just passed. He desperately wanted Lovina to stay, but he understood her position was difficult. With constant reminders daily of her parent's death, he could only imagine the heartache she must feel living here.

Two weeks later, the grandfather clock below the stairs began chiming midnight. Lovina knew this was her chance to make her escape quietly, without fear of waking her sleeping neighborhood. She tiptoed down the stairs, their echoing creaks masked by the gongs of the great timekeeper. Her blonde locks fell over her face as she looked down toward the door, her destination on this dark winter night. She brushed them aside and kept moving. Grabbing the already assembled knapsack from its hiding spot, she slipped her pale pink coat over her slender shoulders and on the final stroke of midnight the door clicked shut behind her.

The cool wind bit at her exposed flesh as she crept through the dead of night. She knew that by leaving she was breaking her oath to the Church, but the call of the outside world was just too great. Not even her one true love could keep her from following her dreams. A single tear rolled slowly down her pale cheek as she looked back, back at the friends and family she would no longer see. Back at Jebidiah.

Tearing her gaze away she strove forward. Her hair was now wet with sweat, despite the cold air that stung her face and pierced her lungs. She ran, as fast as she could. Each snapping twig made her heart jump. Every sound around her made her pause for a moment. A moment was all she could spare. Slowly she kept moving, through the woods, following the hidden road to freedom. As she made her way

Lovina found her mind wandering back to all of her most cherished memories with the community and everything she was giving up. The celebrations and family dinners. Just as she lost herself completely in her thoughts a sharp noise snapped her back to reality.

She looked around desperately for somewhere to hide. She could distinguish faint footsteps coming her way. Who could be out here this late, in the cold? Lovina was convinced that she was caught. Someone had overheard her speaking of her plan to Jebidiah, or worse he had outed her himself. She threw her knapsack into a large bush to her left and jumped behind. As she crouched on the ground crazy accusations filled her head, but she kept her blue eyes focused on the clearing before her. Was it Jebidiah who let slip her secret plan, or did someone else overhear? When a shadowy figure finally caught her eye in the woods, she waited with baited breath to identify her stalker.

Branches crunched beneath his feet as the man emerged into the grassy clearing, uncloaked by the light of the moon. Lovina's jaw dropped and her heart raced at what felt like a thousand beats a second. She no longer needed to hide, she no longer had any fear or doubt about the path that she had chosen.

"Jebidiah!" she exclaimed, sprinting as fast as her legs could carry her toward him. A smile exploded across his face as she jumped carelessly into his outstretched arms. Jebidiah wrapped his muscular arms around her. He grasped her as tight as he could, never wanting to part again. She let her body melt into his. There they stood, nestled in each other's arms for several moments before severing their sensual embrace.

"I could not let you go, Lovina. I love you." Jebidiah confessed. She stared into his beaming blue eyes, looking down upon her. There was only one thing that she could respond.

"I love you too," she answered. Her eyes welled up with blissful tears that soon began running, one by one, down her soft cheeks. Jebidiah reached forward and wiped them away with his calloused hands. One of her arms drew back, reaching up to run her fingers through his mess of tangled hair, damp with sweat. Still stunned by his sudden appearance, she was nothing but ecstatic to see him.

At that moment, Jebidiah leaned down and kissed her soft, cherry lips for the first time, basking in the cool blanket of moonlight penetrating the canopy. Lovina could not believe her luck as she stood in the middle of the trees, in the arms of her love. She had been sure, not hours ago, that she had lost the love of her life forever. Now, she was on her way to making a new life for herself, in a new world, with the man of her dreams.

She leaned in closer to his warm silhouette, grasping at the fabric of his coat. She savored his touch, something she thought she had lost forever in the sands of time. His hand brushed her now flushing cheeks. He traced down her neck and over her petite shoulder. Her hand found its place against his pounding chest. And hers against his.

Jebidiah brushed a lock of hair from Lovina's ear.

"We must go now," he whispered softly to her. Stepping back from him, she nodded in agreement. She would no longer need to start her new life alone, they were together at last. He picked up her knapsack and hauled it onto his back.

"Come," he ushered Lovina back onto her path. Toward the city for the last time. As they neared the bustling hub, she witnessed the blanket of light illuminating the town. Never had she seen something so beautiful. Never had she felt so free.

ADA

Chapter 1

Ada looked at the letter she held in her hands. Her heart was beating hard. Part of herself was questioning the idea of even doing this. She was going to leave behind everything familiar, as terrible as it might be right now, for a man she had never met before. However, his letter and all his previous ones had looked kind enough.

"Ada,

It will be a pleasure to meet you. I have enjoyed conversing with you, and I will be waiting to meet you in the train station on the tenth of October. I hope you will have a safe journey.

Rainer"

While Rainer was usually a lot wordier, their letters had become shorter as they worked out the details of her travel.

"Dear God," Ada said, praying aloud as she finished packing her trunk. "I think you have really given me something special with Rainer. I pray that you would please help me have a safe journey and take away these fears that are plaguing me. Thank you for your mercy. Amen."

Ada sat on her bed as she stared at her trunk. It was not often that a women left a well settled Eastern town to go out West on the idea that they were going to marry a strange man, but Ada had always been one for adventure. Besides, leaving this town behind would let her leave her secret behind. There was no way it could follow her.

Ada took a deep breath. She would soon be able to leave everything behind. The trunk seemed to be full of everything she would need. She didn't even need to look around her room. It was completely empty. She had entered the house with only this trunk of things, and she had not had an opportunity to acquire any new belongings. Ada had already informed her landlady that she would be leaving. The woman had inquired about where she was going, but Ada had skirted around the answer. It was better that no one knew; her landlady tended to enjoy talking about the most interesting bits of news in regards to her tenants a bit too much for Ada's taste.

Ada smiled at the pile of letters she had from Rainer. They had been conversing over two months' time, and she felt as though she already knew him.

"Now, I just need to wait until my train leaves," Ada said, as the hours stretched before her. There would be no one to take leave of.

The next morning, Ada was happy to finally board the train. She had never been on a train before, and she was excited to see what it was like. She smiled to herself as she imagined what Rainer might look like. She had asked him to describe himself, but he only said that he had dark hair and dark eyes. Ada felt like her heart might recognize the man she had met through the letters. After all, if everything went well, they were to be married.

Ada's heart raced. Was she ready for marriage? She had to be. This was the only way to escape her hometown.

"Where are you going?" The woman sitting across from her asked amiably. Her voice startled Ada, and Ada put her hand over her heart.

"I'm sorry. I was completely distracted," Ada said. She smiled. "I'm going to Topeka, Kansas. And where are you going?"

"Denver, Colorado. My journey should be a fair bit longer than yours."

Ada smiled. "Are you visiting or moving?"

"Visiting," the woman nodded. "I grew up in Denver, but I wanted to move East when I got old enough to go out on my own."

Ada smiled. This woman had wanted to move East, and Ada had wanted to move West, each one escaping from where they had grown up. "I'm moving," Ada offered. "I grew up in. . . New York, but it was time for me to move on."

The woman smiled. "Well, I wish you good luck. Moving to a new part of the country can be a very difficult venture."

"Thank you," Ada said, her stomach rolling over. Perhaps it had been difficult for this woman, but anything would be better than her life in New York. She would finally be free to be herself and start over.

Ada passed the journey looking out the window and eating occasionally, but the hours stretched on. Ada felt as though she would never arrive in Topeka.

"What time should we arrive in Topeka?" she asked a man working on the train the next day.

"We are running a little behind schedule," the man said, glancing at his wristwatch. "I think we should arrive any time between four and five o'clock this evening."

Ada nodded. She hoped Rainer wouldn't mind waiting so long. She knew that she hated waiting, but at least when she was on the train, time seemed to pass more easily. However, her body was aching from spending the night sleeping in a sitting up position. Ada just wanted to arrive and sleep in a nice bed.

"I'm sorry," Ada said, stopping the same man as he made another round through the train. "What time is it?"

"1:30," the man replied.

Ada nodded. "Thank you." The time was passing more quickly than she had thought it would. Although lunchtime had already passed, Ada didn't feel the least tinges of hunger. She wondered how Rainer would act upon meeting her. Would he be affectionate right away or more cautious? Ada was naturally cautious, but she felt as though she already knew this stranger.

However, when it was time for Ada to deboard the train, what she saw was nothing like anything she had imagined.

Chapter 2

Ada scanned the crowd. She had never even seen a photo of this man. She assumed they did not have the kind of equipment out here in Topeka to even make a picture. However, there was one man in the crowd who just made her smile. He had dark hair, but Ada couldn't see his eyes. He was taller than a majority of the people.

Ada's heart fell as soon as she saw him talking to a woman. It couldn't be Rainer then. Ada took a deep breath and scanned the crowd again. She shouldn't be disappointed. Why was she disappointed? She had no right to feel disappointed just because Rainer wasn't the first handsome man she ran into.

There were two other men on one side who both had dark hair. One of them could easily be Rainer, but they weren't looking in her direction. Shouldn't they be looking for her? Was she supposed to approach random men and ask if they were named Rainer? This was ridiculous.

Ada let her eye wander back to that first man. He was looking right at her. He smiled and started striding over to her.

"Are you Ada?" he asked.

Ada's heart leaped, and the smile that popped onto her face was involuntarily. "Yes, I'm Ada. You must be Rainer then?"

The man nodded and awkwardly offered his hand. Ada felt strange shaking this man's hand like they had just made a business deal, but a hug would certainly not be appropriate at this time.

"It is such a pleasure to meet you," Rainer said. He looked down at her trunk. "Do you have any more things?"

"That's everything," Ada replied.

"Let's go then," Rainer said, turning and looking back. Ada saw that the woman she had first seen talking to Rainer was still standing there next to a pile of her things. Ada had assumed that Rainer was simply talking to her to find out if she was Ada. If that wasn't the case, why were there two women here for Rainer?

Ada wanted to ask, but she didn't feel comfortable enough yet. Instead, she asked a different question. "Where are we going?"

"I thought," Rainer said, turning back to look her full in the face. His face was chiseled and clean shaven. Ada liked the way he looked. "I thought I would take you to my mother's house. She has offered you a place to stay. I just finished constructing my own cabin, but I don't think it's quite a home yet. I thought letting you stay in my mother and father's house would be a good place for you as we get to know one another."

Ada had heard horror stories about men who had met their women in the stations and married them that same day. Ada was glad that Rainer wanted to take his time. "I think it sounds very thoughtful of you to have planned this out," Ada said. She smiled up at him. "I'm ready to go with you."

Rainer scooped up Ada's suitcase and led her back over to the other woman.

"Ada, this is Kaya. Kaya, this is Ada."

"Pleased to meet you," Kaya said.

"You as well," Ada said, dropping a curtsy. Kaya stared at her strangely, and Ada wondered if her customs were out of place in this Western town. Ada desperately searched for a reason that this woman was going with them. Perhaps she was a family member. Rainer grabbed one of Kaya's bags, and she carried the smaller bag with her.

"I'll drop you off first, Kaya," Rainer said as he placed the suitcases in the back of his carriage. "Let me help you ladies up." Kaya bustled in to be let up first. Ada demurely followed behind. Rainer hoisted her up just as he had done for Kaya. He then went to the opposite side of the carriage and took the horses' reins. Kaya was in the middle.

Ada started becoming angry. She was supposed to be coming out to Topeka to meet a ranch owner who was free to marry. What then was this other woman doing here at the same time? Surely, Rainer had not been writing to more than one woman? Ada couldn't bear the thought. Returning to New York simply was not an option.

"How far do you live from the station?" Ada asked. She leaned forward a little so she could see Rainer around Kaya.

"It's not far. About half an hour's journey." Rainer immediately turned to Kaya. "The hotel is about ten minutes from here. I promise you that the owners are very friendly. I know them personally, and you will feel quite comfortable there."

Kaya smiled at Rainer, and Ada seethed. She was normally a very laid back person, but this woman was coming in and stomping all over her fairy tale. What was she supposed to do? Push Kaya out of the carriage and slide over next to Rainer? Ada shook her head and took a deep breath. She silently prayed and asked God for patience. She asked him for some of his mercy on this girl.

Ada felt a lot better after giving God her worries. The ride was short, and a few minutes later as the carriage rested on the edge of town, Rainer jumped out. He helped Kaya down then gathered her bags.

"I'll be right back. I'm just going to take these bags inside for Kaya. Will you be alright waiting here?"

Ada nodded, feeling the jealousy cropping up. Rainer started walking toward the hotel. Kaya stayed behind for a few minutes.

"Are you courting Rainer?" she asked in a low voice.

Ada paused. Were they courting? It was more like something more. They already knew they were going to get married. "Not exactly," Ada said, trying to explain. "I came to Topeka. I just met him, but. . ."

Kaya nodded. "Okay, I should probably go." She pointed at the hotel across the street. "Rainer is probably waiting."

But we're going to get married! Ada wanted to shout at Kaya, but Kaya was already bustling inside. Ada folded her arms and waited as the sun sank below the horizon. The sunset was beautiful, but Ada didn't enjoy it. She tried to reason with herself, but her idea of a happy ending seemed to be fast fading. She didn't want Kaya getting in her way, and she didn't know how long Kaya was planning to be here. Kaya's open question made her intentions clear enough.

Chapter 3

When Rainer got back in the carriage, all of the things that Ada wanted to say to him, warning him about Kaya's possible intentions were fading out of her mind. After all, even though she had come out here to marry Rainer, they might not fall in love. He might discover that their personalities were simply too different. After all, he didn't seem very picky or jealous like she was.

"Sorry about the delay," Rainer smiled at her. "I felt bad for her. She said that she didn't know how to find the hotel."

"Of course," Ada said. "It was kind of you to help someone you don't know at all." She emphasized those words to demonstrate the difference between herself and this new woman. "The sunset was beautiful."

Rainer smiled at her. "Isn't it? I love the way God puts a touch of beauty in everything he makes."

Ada smiled genuinely, feeling the stress seep away. "I agree. I'm glad that the countryside is so beautiful. While it is a far cry from what I know in New York, I somehow feel at home here."

"Perhaps it is because God created us to be at home no matter where we are in his world."

Ada liked the way that Rainer mentioned God and talked about him as though he was his best friend. "I know you have a lot of cows and few bulls from your letters," Ada said. "But I want to learn more about your farm." Ada sent him a sideways glance. She didn't have to feign interest. She already felt it strongly. "Tell about what you do every day. You're not confined to a small piece of paper or a telegram."

Rainer smiled. "Well, I love my cows, you know. I might get to jabbering away about them for hours at a time. Just tell me when you get bored."

Ada smiled and agreed. Rainer then began telling her about what he did on his farm, how he milked the cows, fixed the fences, and did anything else required of him. Ada was very interested in how he milked the cows.

"I actually have a boy who comes over and helps me with the milking," Rainer explained. "If you're interested in helping, I definitely need the hands."

"I'm not an expert milker," Ada laughed, "but I would be very interested in trying it out."

"Maybe after a few lessons, you'll find you are a natural."

Ada was disappointed to see them pulling into the drive in front of a log house. "This is my family's house," Rainer explained.

"Where do you live?" Ada asked.

Rainer put his arm around her and pointed to the West. "If you look, you might be able to distinguish my house against the moon's light."

Ada was more focused on how his arm felt around her shoulders. She tried to find the house, moving her face around. "I think I see it," Ada said, even though she wasn't sure.

"It's about another fifteen minutes from here by road, unless you get to galloping on a horse."

"Now horse riding is something I can do," Ada said. She was thankful for the horse riding lessons she had had when she was young.

"Let's go inside," Rainer said. He brought her into the house and introduced his mother and father. They were just laying out dinner, and Ada's stomach rumbled. That lunch she had not eaten meant she was empty and ready to eat.

Ada tried to be polite to everyone. "Let me get Ada's trunk," Rainer said. "I'll be back." He went outside and briefly left Ada by herself. She smiled at everyone nervously.

"It's nice to have you here," Rainer's mother- Rachel- said.

Ada nodded. "Thank you for being so accommodating. I know it must put you out to have a stranger among you."

Rainer's father, Benjamin, shook his head. "No, I much prefer it this way. It's better you stay here while you and Rainer get to know one another, before you get married and find out that your letters were poor representations of who you really are."

Ada was silent. She could tell that Rainer's father did not approve of their method of finding each other. She merely looked around and noted that the house was mostly quiet. There were no small children. Ada was under the impression that Western families always had a lot of children.

"Do you have any more children?" Ada asked politely.

Rachel nodded. "Yes, we have five children total. Three have married and moved out. Rainer just finished building his own house, and Ella is probably out there with our baby pigs. She is crazy about baby animals."

"How old is Ella?" Ada asked.

"Sixteen," Rachel replied. Ada nodded and looked around the house as she stood awkwardly in the doorway. "Come," Rachel said. "Sit down, and I will serve you a plate."

"Thank you," Ada said. "But perhaps I should wait for Rainer first."

She saw Rachel give Benjamin a look, but she could only guess what was passing between both of Rainer's parents. When Rainer finally came in with his sister in tow, they all sat down and ate dinner. Ada found Ella very friendly, even though she was five years younger than herself. Ada knew that she would get along well with Ella. Now, Ada only had to worry about how things would work out without Rainer.

"I am going to ride over to my house," Rainer said. He made eye contact with Ada. "Would you like to go outside with me for a few minutes?"

Ada nodded and tried to keep the smile off her face. She had been wanting a few minutes to speak privately with Rainer. They sat outside the cabin on two stools. The only light came from the fire inside that leaked light through the cracks.

"Would you really like to help with milking tomorrow?" Rainer asked.

"I would," Ada hesitated. "But my journey has tired me out. I think I may need to sleep late tomorrow. But perhaps the next day. . ."

Rainer nodded. "Of course. Don't worry. Another day will work just fine. How about after I finish everything that needs to be taken care of on the farm, I could drive you into town? If you are missing anything or you find that you need something, we can get it."

"I really don't need anything," Ada protested.

Rainer held up his hand. "Then I shall get you something you don't need. There is a woman in town who makes delicious ice cream. I'd like to get you a cone."

Ada smiled. She liked the idea. "Okay, I'll be ready then."

"Good night," Rainer said. He stood as did Ada. There was a moment of awkwardness as they tried to decide how to say goodbye. They finally both waved. Rainer mounted his horse and disappeared into the darkness. Ada sat outside for a few minutes by herself, thinking over her day. When she started nodding off, she realized she should go to bed before she fell off the stool and hurt herself.

Chapter 4

The next day, Ada waited anxiously for the time when Rainer would arrive. He did not disappoint, and he came over just in time for the midday meal. After they had eaten, he told her he would ready the carriage and take her for ice cream.

"Oh, can't I go?" Ella asked.

Rainer didn't even take a moment to think about his answer. "Of course. I can't keep my baby sister ice cream free."

"I'm not your baby sister."

"Oh, do I have another sister younger than you?" Rainer teased, pretending to look around. His voice dropped as though they were discussing an important, secret matter. "Is Ma going to have another child?"

Ella laughed. "I wish she would, but you know that won't happen. Let me go change into my nice shoes."

"You don't mind, do you?" Rainer asked, turning to Ada.

Ada shook her head, even though she did mind. She had wanted to experience this first outing alone with Rainer. She felt as though if she went out with brother and sister, she would immediately feel let out of all their jokes.

"Let's go," Rainer said. Ella hurried toward the carriage, but Rainer purposely boosted Ada first before helping his sister in. Ada felt her cheeks warm as Rainer pushed into the carriage and sat right next to her. She could feel his leg pressed against hers, and Ada swallowed a few times to keep her mouth from growing dry.

Rainer teased Ella about her money for ice cream, asking her how she planned to buy one when she didn't have any money. Ada smiled. These two were close, and that said something about Rainer. Ada knew there were seven years between the two, but she liked how close they were. She liked the jokester, generous side of him that she hadn't quite been able to grasp through his letters.

When they reached town, Rainer helped them both down. He walked in the middle and held his arm out. Ada looped her arm through Rainer's and smiled as they chatted. The more she talked to him, the more she felt as though this was the kind of man she could spend the rest of her life with.

They reached the ice cream parlor and stepped inside. The parlor only offered five different flavors and was very different from the pharmacy where Ada got her ice cream in New York. She looked at the flavors and knew immediately that she wanted chocolate. Nothing else appealed to her. Even though there were not a menagerie of flavors, Ella took perhaps ten minutes scanning the flavors.

"What are you getting, Ada?" she finally asked.

"Chocolate," Ada answered easily. "I love anything chocolate, and I probably indulged in it too much in my earlier days." Ada stopped herself before she went too deep into her memories.

"I think chocolate is a good idea," Ella said. "I'll have chocolate as well," Ella said. Rainer ordered their ice creams and handed each of the cones to them paired with a gallant bow.

They sat down at a small table and began eating their ice cream. Rainer and Ella began talking about some of the latest town news. Ada listened in.

"I'm sorry," Rainer said, in the middle of saying something to his sister. "We must have been boring you incredibly. I didn't mean to make conversation about something you wouldn't know, but. . ."

"Please," Ada said, smiling. "Don't worry yourself about it. I am finding it quite interesting learning about my new town."

"So," Ella broke in. "Are you two really going to marry just because you wrote letters to each other?"

Ada's cheeks turned red. This was one of those questions that made the person speechless when they received it, but later on, they knew exactly how they would answer. Ada slid a look at Rainer who was smiling at her. "I guess that's what we're going to find out, Ella. Maybe you should keep your nose in your own business."

Ella gave her brother an annoyed look. "I just wanted to know. It seems a little strange to me."

"You seem a little strange to me," Rainer replied, ducking from his sister's retaliation. Ada stood and threw her napkin in the bin.

Rainer copied suit and held out his arm for her to use once again. Ada slipped her hand into the crook of his elbow as Ella caught up with them. "Did you discover you needed anything?" Rainer asked.

"Um, no, I have everything," Ada said, feeling strange about Rainer's freedom to spend money on anything she might request.

"Surely you need something. Perhaps you and Ella can go together into the general store. I do need to buy some meat. My icebox is almost empty. I shall leave you two here and meet you back in half an hour. Surely you can find something to occupy your time during then," Rainer said.

The two women nodded and watched Rainer took off with a purposeful stride. "Where would you like to go?" Ella asked.

Ada shrugged. "You know this town much better than I do. I might simply like to walk for a bit." The two girls got to know each other as they took a walk through the town. Ada enjoyed meeting new people. Many seemed to know Ella, and they all asked who her new friend was.

Ada found herself the center of attention. "Has the time passed yet?" she asked Ella. Ella nodded.

"I believe it has. Let's go back. If we are late, my brother won't be happy."

The two made their way back to the corner, and Ada was not happy when she saw who was standing there waiting for them. Rainer was talking with Kaya. Ada set her jaw, wanting to hang back so that Rainer wouldn't notice them. Maybe if they hung back, then she could see how Rainer acted when he didn't anyone was watching him.

Kaya laid her hand on Rainer's arm as she laughed. Rainer was laughing too, and Ada's stomach felt sick. What did he find so funny about this woman? What were they talking about?

Ella burst forward to join the two. "Has it been half an hour already? I feel like the time just flies. Ava and I didn't think you would be here yet."

Rainer nodded. "Yes, but don't worry. I haven't minded the waiting."

Ava hung back. She was really hurt by the fact that the one time that she left Rainer alone, he would start talking with this woman and let her put her hands all over him. She had a right to act hurt, but if she acted hurt, then there was no way she would be able to get Rainer's attention again.

Ava stepped forward. "It's nice to see you again, Kaya," Ava said, resisting offering a curtsy.

Ella looked confused. "You know this woman. I've never seen her before. Are you new in town?" Ella asked Kaya.

Kaya nodded. "Yes, I just came in yesterday on the train." She answered as one would answer an annoying pet that kept barking at her.

"Oh, are you going to be staying in town for long?" Ada was glad that Ella had the courage to ask all the questions on Ada's mind.

"Yes," Kaya nodded. "I just moved here. My family lived her when I was little. I thought it would be a good place to find a husband."

Ava couldn't believe Kaya was so open about her intentions, and even more than that, Ava couldn't believe that Rainer was not disgusted by Kaya's obvious desperation.

"So, you'll be here for a while then?" Rainer asked.

"If all goes well, then I hope to live here for the rest of my life," Kaya said, smiling in a sickly sweet way at Rainer.

Ava made a face then quickly changed her expression to a neutral one. She couldn't have Rainer asking her about why she was so resistant to this woman. Some men simply didn't understand. But then, Ava couldn't believe her ears.

"I'm sure my Ma wouldn't mind if I invited you for dinner sometime. I'll warn her, but I am fairly sure that any evening would be fine. She would hate for a new woman in town to be eating by herself every night."

Kaya smiled. "Of course," she smiled. "Thank you for your invitation. I shall be sure to accept your invitation one evening this week. It's not easy moving back to a town from your childhood. It seems as though most people don't remember me. They know of my parents, but that doesn't make it any easier for me."

Ava watched as Kaya successfully secured it. "I'm sure that is hard," Rainer agreed. "I can't imagine living somewhere far away from my family."

"Well," Rainer said, glancing at his watch. "The meat is going to get warm. We should probably go. I shall talk to you later." Ella and Ava said goodbye as well. As Ava was helped into the carriage this time, she didn't feel as happy as she had when they set out that morning.

Chapter 5

Ava spent the next three days exploring Rainer's farm. "I wasn't sure what I thought about a cattle farm," Ada said.

"Why?" Rainer said, giving her an odd look as though it was strange anyone could have a problem with cows.

"Because," Ada said. She smiled, because she knew how Rainer would react. "I've never seen a cow before."

"What?" Rainer's surprise soon gave way to laughter. "Don't they herd cattle where you live? There have to be fields close to the city."

Ada shook her head. "No. My landlady would buy fresh milk every morning, but the man who sold it didn't bring the cow along with him."

Rainer laughed. "I wouldn't bring my cows along either. I use them mostly for breeding, but when they don't have a baby, why wouldn't I take the milk?"

"Do you sell it?" Ada asked. "I haven't seen you coming down the streets making sales."

"I take it to the general store every morning. Mr. Baines buys it from me and sells it to his customers. I keep some of it to make butter. Do you know how to churn butter?"

Ada shook her head. "No, show me how."

Rainer laughed again. "I don't know how. I know the basic process. It includes a lot of movement, but I don't know the specific techniques. My ma can help you out in that area."

Rainer put his hand on his stomach. "I think my stomach is telling me it is supper time. Are you hungry?"

Ada nodded. She wanted to eat a private dinner with Rainer, but he always ate dinner at his ma's house. Ada wasn't quite sure why he had moved over there if he was going to spend some much time there.

They paused in the doorway of his house, and Ada looked around. As soon as she had first seen the house, she began imagining how she could put some touches of home in it. Ada turned back. Rainer was right behind her, and Ada smiled gently.

"When we live here," she ventured to say. "I will make you a special dinner every night."

"You will, will you?" Rainer asked, his thumb coming up and gently stroking her jaw. The touch made Ada feel nervous. She knew that she felt strongly for Rainer, but she had been unsure of his feelings until that very moment. "I think I'll enjoy that very much, a special dinner for the two of us."

"What do you like to eat?" Ada said, taking Rainer's rough hand between her own. She didn't want to go yet. She didn't want to walk across those fields and enter his mom's house, missing this romantic moment.

"My favorite? Oh, I love some good mashed potatoes with some homemade butter. That's my favorite." He looked down at her, and Ada suddenly realized how close they were standing. "But anything you cook, I would be happy to try."

Ada felt her breath come quickly. She looked down at Rainer's lips and back into his eyes. A smile twitched on his lips. He gently bent down and kissed her lips. Ada leaned into his lips and felt them softly part. When Rainer pulled back, his face was completely serious. But the moment Ada smiled, Rainer's face popped into a smile too.

Ada wanted to say something. She wanted to tell Rainer that his kiss had been everything she wanted it to be. She wanted to ask him when they were going to get married. She had come out here to be his bride, but Rainer seemed content to wait.

"Come on," Rainer said. "My ma will begin to wonder where we are."

Ada nodded and took Rainer's extended hand. They walked hand in hand the distance to his ma's house. It took them twenty minutes, and it took every ounce of Ada's strength not to jabber his ear off. She wanted to keep the silence and replay the moment in her head. Just a few minutes before they entered Rachel and Benjamin's cabin, Ada smiled at Rainer. He smiled at her, and Ada knew they shared a special secret.

When Ada stepped inside and saw Kaya seated comfortably at the table, Ada felt her stomach drop. Rainer let go of Ada's hand and went over to greet Kaya. Ada was cordial, but she could not bring herself to be friendly. Even though she was scolding her own behavior, Ada could not help but be jealous. Rainer seemed to be so friendly with Kaya, and he barely knew her.

"I am so glad you were able to find your way here," Rainer said. Kaya smiled back. She spotted Ada in the doorway and seemed confused, but she continued right on with her conversation with Rainer, not caring how Ada felt. Wasn't Ada going to marry Rainer? Hadn't he said as much? Why would he act so different now?

Ada swallowed as she realized that he hadn't mentioned it since in their letters. Maybe the only reason he hadn't married her yet was that he was distracted by Kaya. Maybe *that* was the whole reason it was taking them so long to "get to know each other."

Ada settled on the corner of the couch, wanting to know everything that passed between Kaya and Rainer, yet not wanting to hear how amiable Rainer sounded the whole time. Ada started worrying about what would happen should Rainer decide not to marry her. Ada felt as if she was choking in the heat of the fire. Ada stood and walked over to the doorway where the cool air was coming in. She couldn't go back to New York. She had already been shunned by her family, what was left of it.

Ada swallowed over and over, licking her lips and trying to make herself feel normal. Would she have to stay in Topeka and watch Rainer and Kaya have children together? Ada stepped outside to brush away the two tears that rushed out without permission.

"God," Ada said quietly. "Please, please." She didn't know what else to say as she begged God for mercy on her situation. "I can't go back, but I wouldn't have the money to stay here. I used up almost everything staying with the landlord in New York. Please have mercy. I thought this was what you wanted for me."

Ada was silent and felt a gentle breeze that seemed to come straight from heaven to her. It helped her feel peaceful. It was as though that wind carried the words "Trust Me."

"I'm trying," Ada protested, then she realized she wasn't really trying at all. She had just assumed that everything was going wrong, so she began to let her fears take over. "God, help me trust you," Ada said. She took a deep breath and was just about to step inside when she saw Rainer standing in the doorway.

"Is everything alright, Ada?" he asked.

Ada nodded, trying to force a smile for him. Rainer's smile was not forced by any means. "Come on," he said. "My ma has dinner ready, and she doesn't want it to get cold. You're hungry, aren't you?"

Ada nodded as Rainer took her hand and led her in to a spot on the bench beside himself. Ella and Kaya sat across from them. They all held hands to bless the meal, then Ada began eating. Rainer amiably made conversation with them all. Every time he turned and looked at Ada, she felt warmth in her stomach.

Chapter 6

Ada was disappointed when Rainer offered to drive Kaya back into town. She said that she had asked someone to drive her out there, but she did not have a way back. It was the perfect excuse, of course, but Ada was still disappointed. She did not like the idea of Rainer being with Kaya alone.

Ada dejectedly changed into her nightdress and combed out her hair. She was sharing a bed with Ella, and Ella was getting ready for bed as well.

"If I didn't know that my brother had sent for you to marry him, I would think he was quite taken with that Kaya."

Ella's words were not the ones Ada wanted to hear. Ada nodded, not being able to add her thoughts without crying.

Ella turned and saw Ada's serious face. "Don't worry. My brother's just always friendly to everyone." She seemed to be saying the exact opposite of what she had said only a moment earlier.

"I prefer not to talk about it," Ada said. "I'm very tired, and I need to get up for milking tomorrow." With that, Ada lay down on the bed and shut her eyes, pretending to be asleep.

The next morning, Ada showed up early for the milking. She tied an apron around her waist and made her way out to the barn. By now, she was comfortable around the cows. While she still was scared that one of them would step on her, she didn't shy away from the smell anymore.

"Good morning!" Rainer said, stepping out of the barn.

"Oh, am I late?" Ada asked, her eyes dropping to the ground.

Rainer shook his head. "You're right on time." He came forward and took one of her hands. "Come on, let's get this milking done, so I can let them out to pasture."

Ada sat down on the stool that was set up in her milking stall. Across the aisle, Rainer was milking another cow. His more experienced hands finished three cows in the time it took her to do one, but Ada was learning. She worked out her stress as she finished milking the cow. She needed to talk with Rainer about Kaya. She had to know how Rainer felt. If he felt something for Kaya, she would need another plan, because she couldn't stay in that town either. With about five cows left, Rainer suggested she go inside and make breakfast while he finished up and let them all out to pasture.

Ada quickly whipped up some eggs. She got out the bread she had made the day before and spread some jam on it. She placed the food on the table and waited for Rainer to come in.

"Let's pray," Rainer said. He bowed his head and thanked God for the food then began digging in.

"Rainer," Ada said softly. He looked up. "You know, I've been here more than a week, and we still haven't talked of getting married. I came out here to be your bride, didn't I?"

Rainer smiled at her. "Getting impatient, are you?"

"No," Ada immediately protested. "I just, I'm confused, what with your behavior toward Kaya, and no mention of a marriage."

"Surely you didn't think I wasn't going to marry you," Rainer protested. Ada shrugged. She felt silly admitting it now. Rainer stood and left his breakfast at the table as he pulled her to her feet. He forced her to look into his eyes. "I don't want you to be confused anymore," Rainer said. "Yes, I am going to marry you. I would never bring you away from your hometown, your family, everything, unless my intentions were true."

Ada swallowed, her secret weighing heavily on her. Could Rainer really love her if he didn't know the truth about everything that she had done before she came to Topeka? A part of her whispered that the past was in the past; all had been forgiven. But another part of her was nervous. She was worried Rainer would eventually find out and never trust her again.

Ada pulled Rainer into a hug and laid her head on his chest. She could feel his heart beating. Rainer wrapped his arms around her and gently kissed the top of her head.

"Ada," Rainer said gently. "I will marry you today if that is what you want."

Ada's heart almost felt like it was going to stop beating right then. She couldn't. He had to know, No, he didn't. Ada went back and forth in her mind, and Rainer pulled back from her, easing her chin up as he watched the emotions pass over her face.

"Something's wrong," he said, shaking his head.

This was all wrong! Why hadn't she just agreed as soon as he said it?

"Do you find yourself unhappy here?" Rainer asked, lifting his eyebrows.

Ada shook her head hurriedly. "No, I love your family, and I lo-" Ada broke off. "I enjoy getting to know you. I couldn't imagine my future in any other city with any other family."

"Then, what's the trouble?" Rainer asked.

Ada took a deep breath. She felt the unasked for tears rising to the surface. She was ruining everything! Rainer took another step backward as though her tears were scaring him. He shook his head. Ada wanted to reach out and grab him, force him to hug her again as he had been doing, force him to love her and ignore her secrets.

"I'm sorry," Ada said, quickly wiping her fingers under her eyes. "We should eat up the breakfast before it gets cold."

Rainer sat down at the table and began eating, but Ada found that she could not eat. She stirred the food around on her plate then asked Rainer if he would like some more. He shook his head. "Look," he said. "I know it must be hard being away from your family. If this isn't right for you, you should decide that now before we get married."

Ada's stomach clenched up. She couldn't imagine feeling as strongly about a man as she felt about Rainer, but he seemed to be distancing himself from her. Ada knew that if she wanted to hold onto this man, she would have to tell him everything.

Chapter 7

"Rainer," Ada said, following him to the door. "I need to talk to you."

Rainer turned around and studied her. "What's wrong?" he asked.

Ada wanted to take his hand and pull him back to the kitchen table. She didn't want to have this conversation while he was standing in the doorway, glancing out to the barn, and thinking about his chores. At the same time, she didn't have the courage to be bold and bring him back to the table.

"I am responsible for my sister's death," Ada said.

Rainer raised his eyebrows then did exactly what Ada had been wanting. He guided her back to the kitchen table, and they sat facing each other. "What happened?" Rainer asked.

Ada tried to swallow back the tears, but they seemed insistent on coming anyway. The tears spilled over, and Ada sobbed as she told her story. "It happened about three months ago. The weather was warm, and my mom asked me to watch my younger sister. Penelope was her name." Ada swallowed slowly as Rainer put his hand on top of hers.

"I decided to take her swimming. We stopped by my friend's house. I asked her if she wanted to come. She came with us. Penelope was three years old. When we got to the pond, there were plenty of children who had the same idea. I shooed Penelope into the water, preferring to talk with my friend instead of watching her. I heard children's shouts and saw Penelope in the middle of the pond. She went under the water. I know now, it must have been the tenth or twelfth time she went under. She was drowning. I stood watching her. I wasn't able to move. I counted the seconds, waiting for her to come up. She never did. I finally swam out and found her. . .her body. She was dead."

Ada was crying, and she lost her ability to talk. She laid her face on her hands and sobbed. How could she have been so thoughtless? If she had just looked at her sister instead of her friend, if she had been more careful, or moved more quickly, she could have saved her. Rainer wrapped his arms around her, but it didn't make Ada feel any better.

When her sobs had finished wracking through her body, Ada looked up and wiped her face. "My parents told me I was not welcome in their house any longer. I had to move out. I wanted to come here to escape. I enjoyed talking with you through our letters, but," Ada swallowed, wanting to tell the truth completely. "Honestly, I did not care who the man was, as long as I could get away from my hometown and start over. I didn't like the people looking at me and whispering. I wanted to be normal, accepted, and loved."

Rainer gently rubbed the top of her hand. He didn't look angry or condemning. He looked like he might understand her. "Ada," he said, causing her to look into his eyes, urgently hoping he would be able to forgive her.

"I would never hold such a mistake against you," he said. "What happened was an accident, not something you purposely did."

Ada furrowed her brows.

"I'm sure you loved Penelope, am I right?"

"I never showed her how much I loved her," Ada said, her voice full of regret. She suddenly gave a sob that had a smile. "I remember how she would get home from going out with either me or my mother, and she would throw her shoes into the air and begin running around the house. She hated shoes."

Rainer smiled. "They can be quite cumbersome for a little child."

"I just," Ada was back to thinking on her current situation. "I want to start over. I didn't want you to know. I felt like you might decide I wasn't ready. But, since I came here, I realized that I don't only like the idea of leaving my town, I really like you."

Rainer kissed her forehead. "You know what, Ada? I like you as well. In fact, I really want to marry you."

"Marry me," Ada repeated the words like a child fascinated with the idea. "Yes, please," Ada said.

Rainer stood and took both of her hands. He pulled her closer and kissed her lips with such promise that Ada was left breathless.

"Yes," Rainer said. "I'll marry you. You can be my wife, and I will be your husband. We can have a family together."

Ada smiled widely. "Yes," she said. She hugged Rainer tightly. She wanted to shout. She felt so filled with joy. "We will get married and have a life together."

"Forever and ever," Rainer whispered gently. "Ada, would you have time in your busy day today to go to the courthouse?"

Ada's stomach dropped as she nodded. This was really happening. She was going to marry this man. "I think I can perhaps make time for you," she teased, her fears relived from having told him her darkest secret.

"Do you have something special to wear?" Rainer asked.

Ada nodded. "Yes, I have a special white dress that I sewed myself."

Rainer smiled. "Tell my Ma and Pa to drive you into town. I will meet you at the courthouse at ten o'clock."

Ada wrapped her arms around Rainer and smiled again, delirious with joy. "I shall tell them right now." She took a few running steps toward his parents' cabin before she turned back. "I forgot something." Rainer looked confused for a moment, but then Ada kissed him, her soft lips pressed against his. She pulled back, and he was smiling widely at her.

"I'm going to marry you," Ada said.

Rainer nodded. "Yes, you are. Now, go. Go get ready!"

AMISH LONELY

MONICA MARKS

"Greta, do you truly need another?" Jane Hershberger asked her oldest daughter, her dark eyes barely masking her distain as Greta leaned across the table. Humiliation colored Greta's face and she dropped the roll back into the basket as if it scalded her fingers.

"No, *Mam*," she whispered, sitting her full figure back against the chair. The wood groaned slightly at the motion. Jane nodded approvingly, seemingly unaware of the scowl her other daughters cast her. She turned to her other children, staring at their plates critically.

"Sarah, you must eat," Jane chided, turning to her youngest. "You are becoming too thin. Your body will not withstand childbirth when you are married if you continue to lose weight."

"Greta eats enough for all of us," Noah joked before Sarah could speak. Both Miriam and Sarah kicked him under the table and he yelped.

"Apologize to Greta," Sarah snapped. "Shame on you for mocking her for eating. That is not how a family behaves."

Jane's eye narrowed at her willful daughter.

"Firstly, mind your tone when addressing your elders. Secondly, we are not mocking her, Sarah. We are concerned for her weight. It is not healthy and she is without any potential suitors because of all the excess weight she carries. It is not natural that you and Miriam are betrothed before her. She is the oldest."

An uncomfortable silence overcame the table as the sisters stared at their plates but Noah laughed.

"That's good, right, Mam? You'll always have someone to work the farm with you."

"Noah, shut up!" Sarah snapped. "Do you ever stop talking?"

"Sarah, apologize to your brother," Jane ordered, shocked. "Such language and at the dinner table."

"I will apologize to Noah after you apologize to Greta!" Sarah retorted, rising to her feet. Greta blinked away a sudden onset of tears and forced a smile.

"Please, please!" she cried with forced cheer. "I am not upset. *Mammi* is right; I have become quite large. She is only trying to help."

"There are nicer ways to help," Sarah muttered, shooting her mother a baleful look. Jane was seething.

"You may retire to your room without supper," Jane hissed, pointing a long finger toward the back stairs. Sarah smirked, tossing her napkin angrily against her plate.

"And I thought you just said I was getting too thin."

"Out!" Jane bellowed but Sarah was already on the steps, her dress brushing against the wood of the stairs like a whisper.

"She has her father's sharp tongue. I loved the man but I do not miss listening to his filthy outbursts."

Red faced, Jane returned to her meal but only she and Noah continued to eat. Miriam glanced furtively at her sister but Greta's eyes remained on the table. She could feel Miriam's sympathetic gaze and it made her feel worse.

They pity me, Miriam and Sarah. Poor, fat Greta. Can't find a husband and all she does is eat.

Greta could not help but feel envy when she looked at her two younger sisters, their long dark hair and tiny waists. They had high cheekbones and proud chins, unlike Greta whose face seemed an indistinguishable blob with a nose and two inquisitive brown eyes in the center.

"Greta, if you have finished, you may clean the table," Jane told her daughter. Greta nodded, rising but Miriam jumped to her feet first.

"Leave it, Greta. I will do it," she offered, her hands already collecting plates from the table. "You have an early morning tomorrow at market. You should get rest."

Jane nodded in agreement, smiling warmly at Miriam. There was no doubt that the middle child was their mother's favorite, regardless of what she said.

"Yes, that is fine, Miriam. You are a lovely girl, so kind and beautiful. Greta, remember that kindness is more important than attractiveness for what is inside will shine on the outside. That does not mean you should ignore your health, however."

Miriam's jaw locked at the backhanded compliment but Greta smiled tightly.

"But when all goes well with you, remember me and show me kindness," Greta intoned and Jane looked up sharply, her mouth thinning into a fine line. She did not appreciate her daughter's bible quote choice.

"Good night, Greta," she said flatly, pushing her chair back and whirling about. Miriam smothered a smirk and hurried off after her, leaving Greta alone with Noah. Her small brother glanced furtively at the kitchen and then at Greta's distressed face. He leaned forward and snatched a roll from the basket, tossing it at her.

"Eat it quickly before *Mam* gets back," he ordered and Greta obliged, giving her brother a grateful look.

I may never marry but I will always have the best siblings on God's earth.

"Have a lovely day, Greta," Sarah called, tripping down the front stairs in her night clothes as Greta fastened her cloak about her shoulders. It was a crisp autumn morning, apt to warm up with the rising of the sun but still quite cold at the break of dawn.

"Why are you up so early?" Greta asked, her brow furrowing as she glanced at the clock in the hall. It was not yet six a.m.

Sarah smiled and Greta cringed inwardly. She could read the compassion in Sarah's face and she was not certain she wanted to hear a motivational speech from her well meaning youngest sister.

"Greta, I wanted to see you off this morning and tell you..."

Greta forced herself to focus on Sarah's lips, trying not to notice how slender was her neck.

Why was I burdened with a fight with my weight while my sisters are naturally petite and trim? I wonder if I, too, have a neck under this excess skin, Greta mused with sadness. She turned her dark eyes toward Sarah who looked uncomfortable.

"What is it, Sarah?" she prompted, trying to smile encouragingly. "Is something troubling you?"

"I...I have been reading about ways to rid oneself of excess weight and I just wanted you to know that I can help you if you wish to pursue that avenue," Sarah blurted out. A wave of conflicting emotions washed over Greta and she stared at her sister. Hurt and embarrassment mixed with a bittersweet affection permeated her body.

She does not want people to call her the sister of the barn pig, Greta thought acridly.

Sarah turned bright red and hung her head as if reading Greta's expression clearly.

"I – I do not mean anything – I mean you are beautiful, Greta, just the way you are..."

She trailed off and Greta felt a stab of guilt as she saw the agony in Sarah's dark eyes.

Shame on you. She meant no harm by her offer. She wants you to be happy, not fat and desolate.

"Thank you, Sarah. I will let you know if I would like to try those ideas," Greta said gently, wanting Sarah's face to return to its normal fair color. It seemed ready to pop clear off her head it was so crimson. Sarah nodded quickly and turned back for the stairs.

"Have a good day," she whispered and Greta could tell she was about to cry. She watched as Sarah disappeared up to the second floor.

She may mean well but I am not drinking wheat grass and running laps around the farm, Greta thought, leaving the house for market. *What difference will it make? I am not beautiful and no one will want me even if I was elegant and graceful.*

Miriam and Sarah burst into the barn, startling Greta. Her hands tightened on the cow's udder. Angel mooed furiously and Greta ran her hand soothingly against her black hide in apology. She faced her sisters, annoyed.

"You should know better than to burst in like that during milking," she chided them but their faces were lit with excitement. "Angel will not produce if she is under stress."

She noticed the expressions on her sisters' faces.

"Why are you looking at me like that?"

Without speaking, Miriam thrust an envelope toward Greta.

"What is this?" she asked.

"We don't know!" Sarah squealed. "Open it!"

Greta wiped her hands on her apron and adjusted her prayer bonnet, grinning slightly to herself.

Only in the Amish community would a handwritten letter of unknown origin cause such a fuss, she thought wryly.

"Do you recognize the calligraphy, Greta?" Miriam asked as she peered at the writing. It was simply addressed to Greta Hershberger. She shook her head. The penmanship was not familiar but she did not have occasion to read the writing of many people outside of her immediate family.

"Open it!" Sarah urged and Greta laughed, swatting her sister away as she tried to grab at it with a slim hand. Greta carefully tore open the outer shell, her heart beginning to thump in anticipation.

Who could it possibly be?

For a fleeting moment, Greta's mind wandered to Rueben Mast and she wondered if it was him. Rueben had left the district the previous year to explore his options outside of the community. At first, everyone had been certain that he would return in a couple of months, ready to give himself to the community but months had turned to over a year. Greta found herself thinking of his bright blue eyes from time to time, wondering if he would ever decide to commit to the *Ordnung.*

He has been gone so long now, I do not think he is coming back, *she* thought, a small bout of melancholy touching her heart. She had always felt a deep, inexplicable connection to Rueben. They had been in school together as children and while they did not spend much time together as adults, Greta had always hoped to sneak a peek of him while going about her day or when visiting Middlefield.

She had caught a glimpse of him at market the previous day and he had waved enthusiastically at her from a distance but he was with a group and that was as close as she had gotten to him in months. For some reason, she had lay awake, thinking of his easy-going smile and dimples. Her heart racing now, Greta pulled the paper open and scanned to the end for a signature. Her pulse slowed in disappointment.

"Who is it from?" her sisters demanded in unison. Greta's brow furrowed, perplexed.

"I do not know," she answered slowly. "It is signed 'Ivan Graber'. Do we know an Ivan Graber?"

The sisters stared at each other blankly.

"What does it say? The suspense is too much to bear!" Sarah cried. Greta began to scan it but Miriam snatched it.

"You cannot keep this to yourself. Read it aloud!"

Greta tried to retrieve it but Miriam danced backwards, reading the letter.

"Dear Greta," Miriam began. "You do not know me but I feel as if I know you. Bishop Stoll has told me much about you and I would very much like to meet you. I am told that we have several things in common. I live in Ashland county and I would like to meet you in person. If you would agree, I propose we meet in Middlefield after worship on Sunday. There is a coffee shop at West High Street and Elm. I will be there at 4pm."

Miriam dropped the sheet of paper by her side, her face alight with joy.

"Oh, how romantic!" she shrieked, jumping forward to embrace her sister. "You have a secret admirer!"

Sarah jumped into the embrace, the younger sisters bouncing like sugar induced children.

Laughing, Greta wriggled free.

"Why are you acting so silly?" she demanded, grinning happily. Their good spirits were infectious. Her sisters joined in her laughter.

"You have to admit this is charming, Greta," Sarah said slyly. "He sounds sensitive and intelligent."

"How can you tell such a thing from a piece of paper?" Greta demanded but she admitted she was intrigued by its content.

Greta took the letter from Miriam and read it again. It was not a joke; someone had sent it. There was a man interested in courting her.

I must remember to thank Bishop Stoll on Sunday...wait, I cannot go! What am I thinking?

"I am not going," Greta told her sisters. Their mouths dropped to the ground in shock.

"Why in God's name not?" Sarah demanded. "He put his heart out on his sleeve and you are going to reject him without even meeting him? He will be sitting there, pining for you and you will break his heart. That is cruel, Greta and you are not a cruel woman."

It is better that I reject him before he rejects me, she reasoned, looking down at her lumpy shape under her brown work dress. Understanding seemed to strike her siblings simultaneously.

"Greta, the Bishop has spoken to him about you," Miriam told her gently, putting her arm on Greta's long sleeve. "You have nothing to worry about."

"I wonder if he has told him everything," Greta mumbled, pointing at her stocky chest. "Likely not."

Sarah strode forward meaningfully.

"Yes, I am certain the bishop has told him everything. He has told Ivan you are kind, smart, hardworking and love your family."

"That is not what I mean," Greta replied quietly, her eyes staring down at her full frame. Her sisters were silent until suddenly Sarah smacked Greta in the arm.

"You must stop allowing your weight to define you," she snapped, furiously. "It is not who you are. You are a wonderful, compassionate and wonderful woman just as worthy of love as anyone else. You are meeting with Ivan tomorrow and that is the end of it. We have worship at the Troyers tomorrow. They are not far from Middlefield. It is a sign from God. He sent Ivan to you through the bishop and the Troyers are the closet family to Middlefield. What other signs could you possibly ask for? You would be defying God's will if you choose not to go!"

Swallowing, Greta finally raised her eyes and smiled weakly at her sisters. They waited expectantly and Greta finally nodded slowly.

"Alright. I will go but if it goes badly..."

"It won't!" they chorused and Greta watched as they exchanged a gleeful smile.

This was a terrible idea, Greta thought as she sat at the table, sipping an orange juice and staring nervously out the window. She was too early, she knew that but the wait was excruciating. Her hands reached up and smoothed her hair and prayer bonnet. She practiced smiling into a silver knife, checking her straight, white teeth for flaws.

He's not coming, she thought woefully, glancing again at the clock by the window. She was embarrassed; it was only a quarter to four.

You are becoming over-eager. It is not becoming to act like this. By the time he gets here, you'll be a bundle of raw nerves and act foolish in his presence. You must relax if you wish to make a good impression.

Suddenly, she saw a young Amish man walking toward the entrance. He wore his church clothing still, black handstitched pants and a wrinkleless white shirt under suspenders. His prayer cap covered the base of his skull but his hair was blonde mass, tumbling to his shoulders. The bell chimed as he walked into the coffee shop and Greta could better make out intense grey eyes scanning the shop. Her heart jumped as she saw the simple daisy in his hand.

He brought me a flower, she thought, a slow flush creeping up her neck and staining her cheeks.

Ivan looked about, his eyebrows knitting in concentration. His eye finally rested on her sitting at the back of the shop, his face lighting up in acknowledgement. Yet as he started toward her, his expression began to change from happiness to confusion to disappointment. The blush which had found its way to Greta's face turned into one of humiliation. She was frozen in her chair, watching the discouragement in his face as he approached.

"Greta?" he asked and she could hear the hope in his voice.

He is hoping I say no. Perhaps I should and let him go away thinking I never came.

"Yes," she replied, averting her eyes. "Hello Ivan."

He stood uncomfortably, seeming unsure of where to rest his eyes.

"Uh, this is for you," he said, thrusting the flower at her. She stared at it, the gesture no longer seeming lovely but pitiful. She accepted it, swallowing the rock in her windpipe and Ivan slid into the chair across from her.

"So, uh, how was service today?" he asked, his eyes still darting about as if they wished to look anywhere but on her face.

She nodded.

"Fine," she replied, willing him to look at her but he could not bring himself to do it.

A moment of awkward silence ensued and finally Ivan stared at her.

"You are not what I was expecting."

Greta could feel tears stinging her eyes.

What were you expecting? Someone thin and dainty like Sarah and Miriam? I knew this was a bad idea. I must get out of here, she thought desperately, suddenly feeling caged within the confines of the shop. She rose to her feet.

"I am sorry," she whispered, terrified the tears. "I – it was lovely meeting you."

Before he could say another word, Greta fled, her dark church shoes slipping down West High Street as the tears fell to her round face.

"Greta!"

Sarah jumped from her spot on the porch swing, her face pale as she raced toward Greta, stumbling and sobbing.

"Miriam!" Sarah screamed. "Miriam!"

Greta ran toward her sister's outstretched arms, collapsing, her body trembling violently as Sarah stroked her hair.

"Oh, dear Lord, what happened?" Miriam busted through the screen door of the house, rushing toward her sisters.

"He despised me on sight," Greta wailed. "He could not even look at me."

She buried her face in Sarah's slim shoulders, crying like an infant child for her mother.

"That damned fool," Sarah hissed, her face red with anger.

"Sarah!" Miriam chided but Sarah did not care. She was livid with Ivan Graber. How dare he make Greta feel so inadequate. They heard hooves approaching and Greta whipped her head up, quickly drying her face with the palms of her hands.

"Oh..." Miriam murmured. "It is Caleb. I will send him away."

"No," Greta said firmly as Miriam's fiancé approached, peering at the sisters curiously. She turned for the house, not wishing for Caleb to see her tear soaked face. Sarah hurried after her.

Inside the front room, Greta sat on a wingback chair, staring stonily into nothingness.

"He is obviously dim witted, Greta," Sarah told her sister, her voice teeming with fury. "It is good riddance. If you had married him and borne his children, they too, would have been dim witted. You are fortunate. Now you know for certain."

"No," Greta replied, laboriously turning her chocolate eyes toward her youngest sister. "He is not wrong. I am not appealing to look at. It is not his fault. It is mine."

"No, Greta, your physical appearance is not who you are. We go through our lives forsaking the way of the English to live a simple, homespun life. It goes against the *Ordnung* for him to judge you like that based on the outside without getting to know the real you."

Greta smiled mirthlessly.

"You cannot tell the heart to want something it does not. Attraction is important. You cannot simply cut it out, Sarah. It is instinctive."

Sarah glowered, gnawing on the insides of her cheeks and Greta rose to her feet.

"I have changed my mind," she told her sister. Sarah glanced at her blankly.

"About what now?"

"I would like to learn all of those weight loss suggestions you have read about."

Sarah regarded her slowly, her eyes narrowing slightly.

"You should not do this because of some man who rejected you, Greta."

"I am not," Greta replied and she meant it. She had battled with her weight for as long as she could recall. She had dealt with looks from outsiders and ridicule from her own mother. She could not remember the last time she had felt confidence in anything she had done. No, she was going to make a change and it was going to be for her.

"Will you help me?" she implored of Sarah. Her sister's face lost its sneer and she began to nod, a smile replacing the grimace.

"Yes, of course!" she vowed. "We will make a routine and do it together!"

Greta shook her head, her eyes wide.

"Oh no, you cannot! If you lose any more weight, *Mam* will have my hide!"

Sarah burst into laughter and hugged Greta affectionately.

"It will be fun," she promised and Greta believed her.

<u>Two Months Later</u>

"...and don't forget to bring home some honey. The Troyers have kept jars for us and you constantly forget to pick them up at market!" Jane yelled as Greta hurried down the porch steps. She was already late that morning and her mother's chore list seemed to be growing rather than shrinking as she spoke.

"Yes *Mammi*!" she called, jumping into the front of the cart. She shivered against the frigid winter air, rubbing her gloved hands together for warmth before urging the horse forward into Middlefield.

The morning smelled of snow and while the flakes had not begun to touch the ground, the grey clouds threatened to part and wreak havoc on the district.

I hope they have the market well heated by the time I arrive, Greta thought, gripping the reins. She never remembered the winter hitting her so hard before and it was only December. They had not been touched with the brunt of the season yet.

I imagine much of it has to do with the lack of meat on my bones now, Greta thought happily. She remembered the juice which Sarah had prepared for her the night before and Greta pulled out the cup from beneath the seat where she had put it earlier in the morning. It was beginning to freeze slightly but it could still be consumed.

She pinched her nose and took a gulp of the green liquid, shuddering as it went down. It tasted awful but it had worked miracles.

In the past eight weeks, Sarah had devised a rigorous diet and exercise plan for Greta and had adhered to it dutifully, remembering that the result would be. Both her patience and Sarah and Miriam's constant support had begun to pay off. In a short time, Greta found she had more energy and was sleeping better at night. She had lost several dress sizes but most of all, Greta felt a tentative confidence for the first time in her life. She no longer thought about the hurt which Ivan's dismissal had been and instead thought about how the Englishers in the market smiled at her.

At least someone finds me attractive, she thought happily. Of course, she would never entertain the idea of an Englisher; she was a baptized woman, completely devoted to the community and *Gottes Wille.* Still, it made her smile that for once, someone found her appealing on the eyes.

The wagon drew close to market and Greta jumped out to unload the cheeses into a wheelbarrow. As she turned, she drove directly into a man at her back.

"Oh!" they cried in unison and Greta drew the cart back to inspect her victim for damage. The Englisher looked up and Greta's heart caught in her throat.

"Rueben!" she gasped, shocked. His eyes widened, a slight confusion passing over him as he peered at her face.

"Greta Hershberger?" he asked, stepping back. She nodded, smiling sweetly. Greta had not seen him in months, not since the day he had casually waved at her in the busy market.

"Greta, I did not recognize you!" Rueben declared, grinning broadly. "You look wonderful!"

Greta lowered her eyes demurely, deeply flattered.

"I lost some weight," she admitted.

Why did you say that? It is perfectly obvious you lost weight, Greta, she chided herself, cringing slightly. *He is going to think you boastful.*

Yet Rueben was shaking his head.

"Let me take that from you," he offered, taking the handles of the wheelbarrow. Greta raised her eyebrows and smiled.

"No, I can see you have lost some weight but it is something more than that. You have a glow about you which I have never seen. You look..."

"Happy?" Greta offered and Rueben glanced back, laughing.

"Yes, I believe that is what it is. I must say, it becomes you," he added. Greta was sure her cheeks were the color of the apples in the neighboring booth.

"This is you, is it not?" Rueben asked as they stopped at the Hershberger kiosk. Greta nodded, again exalted that he remembered. She had always harbored a deep affection for Rueben and had been disappointed when he left to work in Middlefield. She had secretly hoped he would return but she could see that he was content with his life in town. She desperately wished to ask him if he would ever consider returning to their district but she dared not.

"Why are you here so early?" Greta asked, eager to shift the subject from her appearance. Rueben grinned boyishly and Greta marvelled at how bright were his green eyes.

He is very appealing to look at. Perhaps that is why I have longed for him to return to the district. But Greta knew that was not true. Rueben had never treated her like an overweight outcast. Anytime she had occasion to see him, he had a kind word and quick smile. Sometimes Greta felt as if he was the only person in the world who did not see her as overweight and undesirable.

Or perhaps that is merely wishful thinking, she thought wistfully.

"I am looking at renting a booth here," Rueben replied, pulling her wares from the wagon and helping her set up the table. Greta watched in disbelief as he did a better set up than she did.

You can take the boy out of the Amish but you cannot take the Amish out of the boy, Greta thought admiringly.

"It's a secret," Rueben told her, leaning in conspiratorially. "But I must meet with the rental manager. Will I see you later?"

"I hope so," Greta said. All the blood in her body rushed to her head. She could not believe she said that aloud but Rueben beamed happily.

"Me too," he told her. He waved and disappeared around the corner, leaving Greta to watch after him with longing.

Behind her, someone cleared his throat suggestively and Greta whirled, guilt flooding her at being caught gawking after Rueben like a lovesick puppy. Her eyes widened in surprise.

"Ivan!" she cried. The morning was full of surprises. He smiled sheepishly at her, his pupils dilating as they took in her fine bone structure.

"I was not sure if it was you, Greta," he confessed. "You look..."

"Happy?" Greta suggested.

"Thin," he replied and Greta found herself slightly irritated at the response. Her mind flittered to Rueben who had noticed her inner change immediately. She offered Ivan a timid smile.

"Was that Englisher a friend of yours?" Ivan asked, gesturing his blonde head in the direction where Rueben had vanished. Greta thought she detected a note of jealousy in his voice.

Do not be absurd. What does Ivan have to be jealous of? You would not know what jealousy sounds like if it whispered directly into your ear. When have you ever had occasion to hear envy in anyone's voice?

"He is not an Englisher," she replied easily. "He was a member of our district."

"But he is not any longer so he is an Englisher," Ivan finished and Greta found herself annoyed by the arrogance in his tone. She decided not to pursue it.

"Are you well, Ivan?" she asked and he nodded, his eyes shifting downward.

"Greta, I feel very badly about how things went between us when we met a few months ago. I was rude and you did not deserve such treatment."

Greta was touched by his apology and immediately forgave him.

"You needn't apologize," she assured him. "You were misled as to who I am."

"Who you were," Ivan corrected, his eyes raking about her face again. Greta found herself feeling slightly violated by his expression. She flushed and turned to finish setting up her display.

"Would you be willing to give me another chance?" he asked pleadingly and Greta softened. She nodded slowly.

"Yes," she agreed. "Perhaps we can meet again after worship tomorrow."

Ivan's grey eyes lit up.

"Wonderful!" he declared. "Four o'clock again?"

Greta nodded and Ivan beamed. At that moment, Rueben came around the corner with the rental manager, talking animatedly. Ivan's smile faded as the two approached. They continued to speak as the walked by but Rueben paused to wink at Greta before walking off into the far side of the market.

"I will see you tomorrow!" Ivan bellowed, much louder than he necessary and Greta cringed staring at him strangely.

He said that for Rueben's benefit, she realized, surprised at the childishness of the action. She smiled tightly.

"Until tomorrow, Ivan," she replied. He sauntered off toward his area of the market but Greta found herself straining to catch another glimpse of Rueben but he was gone.

"You agreed to see him again?" Sarah yelped, staring at Greta aghast. "After the way he treated you?"

Greta shrugged.

"Isiah 43:25, I, even I, am he who blots out your transgressions, for my own sake and remembers your sins no more," Greta recited and Sarah sighed, glancing at Miriam who remained silent. The women took their places on their side of the house in the pews which had been transported to the Millers for that week's service.

The Hershberger women hanged their heads and waited for the ministers to take their places but Greta's mind was not on prayer. She had been unable to stop thinking about Rueben Mast since seeing him the previous day. She found herself drifting into a daydream where Rueben saw her, threw up his hands and declared, "What am I doing? I have made a mistake. My place is here in the community with you!"

She was indulging in fantasy of course but it was pleasant to envision.

Mam will be happy now. I have a suitor in Ivan and then she will have all of us married by next year.

Sarah suddenly elbowed Greta in the ribs and she jumped from her reverie.

"Greta look!" she whispered. Greta turned to look at where her sister was pointing and her eyes grew large.

Am I still daydreaming? She shook her head as if to clear any potential of a dream from her mind and watched as Rueben strode into the Miller's living room, greeting the congregation warmly. A din followed his entry and a small crowd encircled him.

"He's back?" Greta asked in disbelief. "Does this mean he's here to stay?"

Sarah, Miriam and Jane had no answer. He had left once before, he could do it again. Greta's heart raced and the ministers and deacon called the service to order.

I will talk to him after worship, Greta vowed.

Greta walked slowly, her mind heavy with thoughts. After worship, Greta was trying to make her way through the throng of people, looking around desperately for Rueben. She had lost him in the crowd and she felt like her heart was going to explode.

I am to meet with Ivan soon but I do not want to pursue a future with Ivan if Rueben is back with us for good. I will not know unless I find him. I must find him!

As the families began to say their good-byes, Greta realized with defeat that he was gone and she had no answers.

It was time to meet with Ivan.

It is unfair to give Ivan the idea that we are courting if I would rather be with Rueben. Greta grimaced. Even if Rueben was home to stay, there was no guarantee that he would feel the same about her.

Ivan is the best match for you. You must forget about Rueben. If he had interest in you, he would have shown it before he left the community. Ivan will make Mammi happy.

She ignored the voice in her mind which asked who would make her happy.

Greta pulled open the door to the coffee shop and Greta walked in. She was suddenly flooded with a memory so strong, it almost brought her to her knees.

In her mind's eye, she relived the look in Ivan's face when he first saw her. The disappointment, the borderline contempt as if she had misled him somehow.

He had no interest in getting to know me as a person. He had already made up his mind when he saw me.

"You are not what I was expecting."

The words still cut into her like a fresh wound, despite her desire to forgive and forget.

In the same booth where she had sat two months earlier, Ivan rose, a smile lighting up his face.

"Greta!" he called. The memory seemed to fog her vision. She froze in her place, her head turning as if by an invisible string. Directly to her right, sat Rueben, smiling up at her, a slightly bemused expression on his face.

"Hello Greta," he said. "Would you like to sit down?"

Her eyes flittered back to Ivan whose face had turned stony as he recognized Rueben. He folded his arms firmly over his chest and glared at them.

"I don't know," she answered honestly. "Do I?"

Rueben chuckled.

"I can hardly make that decision for you," he told her. "But I would enjoy your company. I always have."

The words filled her heart and suddenly Greta knew that he was as smitten with her as she with him.

He genuinely cares about me. He does not care if I am big or small. He cares about what is in my heart.

"Greta!" Ivan snapped. "I have been waiting for you."

Greta shot Rueben an apologetic look.

"I will return in a moment," she promised, stalking toward Ivan, her eyes gleaming.

"Hello Ivan," she said. Relief flittered over his face and he went to slide back into the booth but Greta remained standing.

"Sit down," he urged but Greta shook her head.

"I cannot," she replied and Ivan's brow furrowed in anger.

"Why not?" he demanded. Greta smiled, a feeling of peace crossing over her.

"Because you are not what I was expecting."

Without waiting for a response, she whirled on her heel and joined Rueben at his table.

"I think he is angry," Rueben commented, watching as Ivan stormed from the shop, glaring daggers at them both.

"That is between him and God," she replied, smiling slightly. As she looked at Rueben, her beam began to fade.

"Are you coming home?" she asked hopefully. Rueben sat back in his chair and studied her carefully.

"Is that why you rejected Ivan? Because of me?"

Greta thought about it for a moment and to her surprise, she began to shake her head.

"No," she answered truthfully. "Whether or not you come home or whether or not you choose me, I deserve better than Ivan."

Rueben's eyes filled with adoration and he nodded slowly.

"Yes, you do. You deserve wonderful things."

"You did not answer my question," Greta said, shifting her eyes, disappointment filling her gut. She had a sense that she already knew the answer to her inquiry.

"Yes and yes," Rueben replied, sitting forward and grasping her hands tightly.

"*Yes and yes*?" she echoed. "You are back? You are getting baptized?"

Rueben nodded. Comfort flowed through Greta.

"What is the second 'yes' then?" she asked, catching her breath as they stared at one another. Rueben chuckled.

"Yes, I choose you."

In that moment, all the confidence Greta had ever lacked flooded her body in a sea of warmth. She had never felt more beautiful.

AMISH VALLEY

MICHELLE BENTON

January

You have to stop this! Naomi chided herself, trying to silence what was happening in her head. But she could not stop her foot from tapping and her neck from bopping as she hummed under her breath. *Someone is going to catch you one day and then you'll have some explaining to do.*

She kept her head down so she would not be heard laughing. However, her snickers did not fall on deaf ears and when she turned her head from the firewood she was splitting, two of the women glared at her from their various vegetables.

"Do you find something amusing, Naomi?" Anke Hilty asked coldly but Naomi quickly shook her head and averted her eyes. Still, she could not stop the smile from toying on her generous mouth. She had only been welcomed into the district four months earlier but it seemed that Naomi was still regarded as Englisch to several of the women in the community. Naomi was smart enough to realize that it had little to do with her personally and more to do with upsetting tradition but it did not ease her sense of discomfort. Women like Anke and Anke's sister, Emma made the conversion to the Amish way of life difficult sometimes. If not for Naomi's unstoppable sense of humor, she was sure she would have returned to life in Indianapolis long ago. *I'll be an outsider until I get baptized,* she reasoned, turning her attention fully toward the garden now and forcing any other "English" thought from her head...like the popular song which had been playing over and over in her mind since she had woken at dawn.

"Naomi, you can't be serious!" her mother had screamed when Naomi had told of her plans to convert. "You can't go a day without the internet!"

Naomi had shaken her head, expecting the histrionics from her mother, inwardly relieved to know she would not have to listen to the woman's incessant shrieking day in and day out.

"I can and I will."

"We won't be able to visit you!" her father had protested. "They don't allow for outsiders in their community."

"I know! Isn't it wonderful?" As Naomi spoke, she genuinely meant the words. The Amish way of life, their seclusion, their devotion to each other and God was inspirational to her in every conceivable way.

But it had been Stephen who had almost made her change her mind.

"You can't run away from your problems by disappearing, sis," he told her. "You will just find yourself walking into a whole new whack of problems. But if this is what you want to do, I support you, no matter what. I hope you know I'll miss you."

His words had hit a sour note with Naomi and that night and every night subsequently, what he had said had rung in her head. *I am not running away,* she told herself over and over. *I am trying to under-complicate my very overcomplicated life. It is too messy now, filled with things I do not require. All I need is to surround myself with fresh air, hard work and true, unpretentious, like minded people.* She knew that her family was concerned about her mental state. Ever since her fiancé, Carlos had fled town with her best friend, things had begun to spiral downhill for Naomi. In the aftermath of the betrayal, she had set fire to all his belongings during an onset of uncontrollable fury. She had done so on the front lawn of the house they shared, hoping that Carlos would return and see a pile of ash where his beloved Gucci ties had once been. Carlos had never shown his face at the house again and unfortunately, the act had resulted in an arrest as the flame had spread, damaging the neighbor's car. She had been lucky, let off on probation as it was a first offense and then promptly fired from her job as a personal support worker.

"I'm sorry, Arry, I really am," her boss had told her, regret gleaming in his eyes. "But you can't have an arson record and work with the public, especially not in the medical field."

"I've been working here for four years! It was a stupid act of passion!" Naomi had protested, tears threatening to flow down her round cheeks as her full mouth quivered. "I am no danger to anyone!"

"I know that, Arry and you know that but you know you are required to have a clean record. I can't keep you employed with this agency any more." As he led her away in full blown sobs, he emptily promised to give her an excellent reference but he knew just as well as she did that no one was ever going to hire her again as a PSW. A felony was a felony after all. From there, she had been evicted as she wallowed in depression, eating ice cream and watching Netflix twenty hours a day. Naomi had not a cent in savings and between asking her parents for money and living on the streets, Naomi opted for the latter. She went to stay with Stephen for a short time before having an epiphany one day at the farmer's market; she would join the Amish. At the start, even she had recognized how obscure an idea it was but it did not stop her from investigating. She began frequenting the market more often, discovering that it was almost unheard of for outsiders to convert. Naomi pushed the issue, finding only two people who would entertain her questions. One was a man named Camp Girod, a solemn faced farmer who answered her inquiries in as few words as possible but Naomi soon learned that was his way of speaking and not rudeness. The other was Emma Hilty, a girl who had promised to become a fruitful friendship but had somehow fallen short down the line. Both had seemed happy that she had shown so much interest in their faith and were eager to educate her to the best of their ability. One afternoon, Camp brought the bishop of their district to meet with Naomi to answer some things they did not know. Naomi had almost hugged the tall, shy man but immediately stopped herself. *You must behave like a proper Amish woman from here on in,* Naomi told herself. *No more city girl shenanigans.*

The bishop initially had not been convinced by Naomi but as time went on, he began to recognize her intentions as true and slowly, with

Camp and Emma whispering praise in his ear, he eventually began to take her seriously.

"It is often very difficult for an outsider to simply assimilate into our culture. We don't have the luxuries which your kind seem to deem necessity to function," the Bishop had warned. "More often than not, the English return to the life in which they have been reared."

"That won't happen with me, Bishop!" Naomi declared with conviction. "I will be one hundred and twenty-five percent committed to the community. You'll see!"

The elderly man had raised a bushy eyebrow, somewhat distastefully at Naomi's loud proclamation.

"Naomi, in our community, patience and peace are considered large attributes. The quick tempered and moody do not fare well in our lifestyle," Bishop Kurtz continued. "We are one with God's teaching and he teaches the virtues of the meek. Do you believe you can follow those teachings?"

Naomi nodded eagerly although inwardly she cringed at her own lie. In truth, she had little religious teachings and knew very little about the Bible. She vowed that she would read the scripture from start to finish. *I'll do it in one sitting if that's what it takes!* In the end, Bishop Kurtz decided that Naomi would try the Amish way, largely influenced by Camp and Emma's convincing but partially enthralled by her belief that she was meant to be Amish. Under normal circumstances, the Bishop would not have entertained such an inane idea but Naomi had become a legend in the district and he had finally allowed his curiosity to get the best of him. Every evening after market, one of the parishioners would regale the bishop of tales. A young, bubbly woman would stop by their stalls at the market, begging for information about their culture. Most dismissed her, believing her to be a reporter and not wishing to fraternize with outsiders or disclose anything inappropriate. However, Emma had been amused by her tenacity and began to converse with the girl. She had been pleasantly surprised to discover that Naomi had a genuine desire to forsake the outside world and start fresh within the security of their community. Before long, Camp Girod, whose dairy booth neighbored Emma's meat display, heard the outgoing Naomi and found himself drawn into conversations also. If Emma and Camp had not been such upstanding members of the district, Bishop Kurtz would have never met Naomi Pryce. In the end, however, he was just as smitten with the girl as the other two members of his parish.

On a warm night in September, Naomi, in only a very simply skirt and white blouse, said good bye to Indianapolis and moved into the Hilty's home in rural Indiana with Bishop Kurtz's blessing.

That had been four months earlier. In that time, Emma had lost her good nature with Naomi. Naomi suspected it had much to do with the fact that Anke did not like her. Naomi tried to tell herself it did not matter, that she belonged there just as much as they did. *Just because I wasn't born into this life, doesn't make me any less Amish!* She pep talked herself. At that moment, another popular song blasted into her head. She shook her head mournfully. *My own psyche is mocking me.*

"It's raining on your head, Naomi and yet you seem so content, sitting there in the mud." Naomi whipped her head up and looked at the speaker. Anke and Emma's brother Evan stood above her, his light blue eyes twinkling with laughter. To her surprise, she realized he was right. The sunlight had disappeared and dark rain clouds had overtaken the sky. She suddenly realized that the Hilty sisters had retreated inside without saying a word. Water was seeping into her boots and the air had taken on a sudden chill. She rubbed her hands against her

"Come inside before you fall ill," Evan laughed, offering a hand. She eagerly accepted and followed the oldest Hilty sibling inside the farmhouse. Anke scowled at them from the window and Naomi realized she was still holding Evan's hand. Embarrassed, she pulled her palm from his and he turned, winking at her. Naomi blushed crimson. Evan had bestowed endless attention upon her since her arrival in the district. From the first night, he had told her stories on the porch and introduced her around to the neighbors. In turn, he asked that she tell him about the city, the sights and people. Naomi did her best to make it sound exciting, despite her recollection being less than glamorous but it seemed the more she embellished, the more captivated Evan became. Naomi had almost felt like he had claimed her but of course that was ridiculous. That was something the English would do, not the gentle-minded Amish. Still, Naomi was flattered and relished the friendship she found in Evan.

"Let me make some tea. You should change your clothes. I don't understand how you can be so at peace in the rain," Evan told her. "Especially someone so accustom to having warmth at their fingertips!"

Naomi shrugged. It was difficult not to be at peace in such surroundings. There was no bustle, no stress. The days were long, yes, but Naomi felt as if she had always been tilling fields and saying prayers. She hadn't been certain that the religious aspect would appeal to her, being reared nearly agnostic but the more time she had spent in worship, hearing God's plans, the more Naomi recognized what she had been missing from her life. *You made the right choice coming here,* she told herself as she quickly changed and brushed out her dark hair. She regarded her reflection in the mirror. She was an attractive woman by any standards; shoulder length straight brown hair, her bangs finally growing out from the blunt cut she had worn from before joining the community. Her dark eyes were intelligent and wide, her mouth constantly curved to a smile. Her inner happiness radiated outwardly and she found herself smiling in the glass.

"Are you coming?" Evan bellowed from downstairs. "The tea is becoming cold!"

"Yes!" Naomi yelled back and winced. *You need to tone it down!*

She hurried out of her small room and down the stairs to meet with Evan in the kitchen. Emma stopped her, stepping out from the shadows in the sitting room.

"Naomi," she said in a low voice. Naomi paused in surprise, glancing toward the kitchen but Evan was not standing there.

"You need to stay away from my brother," she warned. "Don't say I didn't warn you." Naomi felt her heart skip a beat. In the darkness of the hall, Naomi thought she saw a glint of anger in the younger girl's eyes. She did not reply, instead backing away, looking hurt at Emma's words, watching the younger girl disappear up the stairs. *I suppose I am not good enough for her brother, then? Am I always going to be an outsider? Will they never accept me here?*

"Naomi, would you care to take a walk with me after supper tomorrow?" Camp asked conversationally after worship. Naomi nodded.

"Of course," she replied, unsuspectingly. "I would love to!"

"There is a matter I would like to discuss with you," he said in his usual somber tone. Naomi smiled to herself but nodded again. She could not imagine Camp being anything but serious. *He probably wants to discuss the winter frost and he makes it sound like the world is about to come to an end,* she thought jokingly. She dared not jest with Camp. He was far too routine for such play. Naomi had once been present when Camp had been unwell and overslept as a result. She had never seen anyone so flustered in all her life. His entire demeanor had been altered and he snapped viciously at everyone in his wake. Naomi had been wounded by his sharp tones until Emma had told her that Camp was the most structured person in their district. From the time he was a child, he had risen with the roosters and planned every single minute of every day down to the second. When his schedule was disrupted, it made him confused and disoriented. After learning that, Naomi had gone out of her way to accommodate his whims. After all, if it had not been for Camp, she likely would never have been allowed in the community. Naomi owed him a debt of gratitude. Also, Camp was one of her only friends. She didn't know why, but Camp seemed to like her.

"You're not like anyone I would ever imagine Camp Giron associating," Anke told Naomi icily one day after Camp walked away. Naomi and he had been speaking over the fence for almost half an hour. Naomi had raised an eyebrow, stung by the connotation.

"And why not?" she demanded. "I am just as God fearing and hard working as anyone here, Anke! I wish you wouldn't imply that I'm not!"

"Maybe so," the older sister had replied. "But you are also the loudest. Camp is a quiet, gentle man. You are so...brash."

"Brash? I am not brash!" Naomi had yelled. Anke had smiled thinly as if to say "I rest my case." Naomi had gone out of her way to avoid speaking with Anke after that but Anke made it easy. She barely had two words to say to Naomi under the best of circumstances. Inwardly, though, she wondered what Camp found interesting about her. *Anke is not wrong. I am exactly the opposite of the man. I always thought that introverts found extroverts exhausting.* Naomi did not have to wait long to find out.

The following evening, the night had turned bitterly cold but after supper, Camp knocked on the Hilty door. Naomi hurried threw on her coat, scarf and gloves before adjusting her bonnet and heading toward the front door to meet her friend. Evan grabbed her by the arm as she went to leave the kitchen, a scowl darkening his fair face.

"Are you going out walking with Camp Giron?" he demanded. Surprised, Naomi nodded at the question.

"Yes," she answered, cocking her head in confusion. Evan's blue eyes narrowed dangerously.

"Is that a problem?" Naomi asked nervously. She studied his face for an answer and suddenly he realized how tightly he was holding her. Abruptly, he let her go, shame flooding his face.

"No, of course not," he told her hastily. "I – it's very cold outside is all. Please dress well." With that he disappeared into the back of the house, leaving Naomi staring after him, open mouthed. *Am I delusional or was that an act of jealousy?* She asked herself, a warm glow of happiness filling her insides. She had suspected that Evan liked her but he had never been anything more than friendly toward her even though the community called his ways flirty. She secretly hoped that he was jealous of Camp. She pushed Evan out of her mind as she remembered that Camp was waiting for her. *You must not make Camp wait,* she thought guiltily but Camp did not look perturbed as he stood in the foyer, chatting with Mrs. Hilty.

"Ah, there you are, Naomi. Please do not be late. We have a very busy morning tomorrow," the matriarch ordered and Naomi nodded obligingly. Naomi had never given the Hilty's any cause for alarm. She had done everything per her agreement with Bishop Kurtz.

"Remember, Naomi," Bishop Kurtz had told her when she had arrived. "It is not what I expect of you but what God and this community expect of you. You will see a reflection of yourself in every action, good or bad. The choice is yours but in the end, it is only you who must answer to God."

"Shall we?" Camp extended his arm and Naomi took it, smiling. The pathway to the road was icy and Camp held fast to her as she almost slipped several times.

"My goodness, Camp," Naomi exclaimed as ten minutes had only seen them a few hundred feet down the road. "Perhaps we should plan our walk for another night."

"I would prefer not to, Naomi if you do not mind indulging me." Naomi smiled and shrugged tolerantly. She could barely feel her face or toes in the extreme cold but she did not want to disappoint Camp.

"This sounds urgent, Camp. Of course, we can speak tonight. What is going on?"

Camp paused and looked down at her, his own dark eyes soulfully deep. He seemed to be thinking about his words and in spite of her resolve to be patient, Naomi wished he would spit it out. She flexed her fingers inside her gloves to ensure they were still there.

"Naomi, I am very proud of the way you have situated yourself in the community," he began. She smiled, abashed by the praise.

"I couldn't have done it without you, Camp. You know that, right?"

"I believe that your perseverance would have paid off regardless of my small role. However, I am happy you are here."

"I am thrilled to be here!" she announced. He nodded soberly and cocked his head.

"Have you given any thought to your baptism?" he questioned.

"Bishop Kurtz has suggested April. Personally, I would like to do it tomorrow but I confess, I never much wanted to join the Polar Bear Club." A look of confusion passed over Camp's eyes and Naomi realized he didn't understand the reference. *You really need to get your head out of the English,* she scolded herself again.

"Anyway, you'll know when I know. I'm pretty sure everyone around here gets an invite, right? Is that what you want to talk about? You're worried I might go back to the city after everything you've done to bring me here?" she asked, smiling. Camp's brow furrowed and Naomi realized that he had not entertained that thought whatsoever, at least not until she had brought it up.

"No..." he said slowly. "That was not what I wanted to speak to you regarding."

He said nothing and Naomi felt a smidgen of annoyance. *I know patience is a virtue but I'm becoming an ice sculpture here!*

"Camp, you're my friend, you know that, right?" He nodded, seemingly more confused by the conversation shift.

"As my friend, probably my best friend here, I am begging you to ask me whatever it is because I am freezing to death! I swear there are corpses warmer than me right now!"

Camp inhaled sharply and nodded.

"I wanted to ask you, if, once you get baptized..."

"Yes?"

"If you would consider giving me your hand in marriage?"

<u>**April**</u>

"Welcome, Naomi Pryce to our community!"

A cheer erupted and Naomi, soaked to her knickers, beamed at the crowd which surrounded her. She noted with pride that even Anke nodded in approval, a thin, funny smile pursing her lips. *I am one of them now! Finally! They can't call me an outsider anymore!* She thought. She turned to Bishop Kurtz and bowed slightly in thanks.

"We are pleased to have you, Naomi. You have demonstrated the loyalty, hard work and patience which we value so highly. If only you would work on your Pennsylvania Dutch..." A small chuckle flew through the group and Evan lunged forward to take her arm.

"Everyone speaks English anyway, *liebchen*. Come on, Arry. Let's eat!" Happily, she allowed herself to be led toward the Hilty barn where a feast had been set up for the baptism. Out of the corner of her eye, she saw Camp standing alone, under a tree, looking forlorn.

Since the frigid night of their walk, Camp had not come calling and Naomi admitted that she missed his company terribly. Of course, Evan was her constant companion, joking and laughing with her, despite the tongue wagging of the community.

"She does not behave properly," some of the older women complained. "She flirts recklessly with the Hilty boy and she lives in that house!"

"He is no better," others countered. "He has been brought up right in this community and he blatantly disregards our traditions. He acts like he has English blood."

But neither Evan or Naomi seemed to mind the gossip. It was not because they did not hear of it; in fact, Mr. and Mrs. Hilty often forbade them to be together alone but they still managed to find a way to see one another and enjoy each other's company. Naomi had been counting the days to her christening. She knew that the moment she officially became Amish, Evan would ask her to marry. *I wonder if he will do it today even,* Naomi thought, peering at him out of the corner of her eye. He returned her look of adoration and impulsively squeezed her hand, not releasing it. Naomi did not take her palm away this time, despite the looks she received from the members. She could almost hear their thoughts; *she just got accepted into the fold and look at her! Acting like a fallen woman!* Naomi did not care. She was incredibly happy and she knew she was about to become happier.

The day progressed beautifully. There was food and banter. The only dark cloud was Camp's almost palpable sadness. She had not outright refused his pre-emptive proposal but she had let him down in a way that he knew she did not see a future with him. *Camp will find someone. He is dependable and hardworking. Any woman in the community would be lucky to have him.* But the thoughts did not alleviate Naomi's guilt and she forced herself to focus on the festivities. As the afternoon wound into evening, she found herself exhausted. The events of the day had taken a toll on her and she wanted to retire early for the evening. She excused herself just after dark and retreated to her bedroom. As she lay in bed, a smile touching her lips, she knew that tomorrow would be the day Evan would ask her to marry him.

"Naomi!" She bolted up in her bed, scared out of a dream state. It took her a moment to reconcile her surroundings and then, through the dark, she peered at Emma and Anke who stood in the doorway, both relief and anger written on their faces.

"What?" she croaked, her throat like cotton. "What happened?"

Emma exhaled slowly and crept into the dark room, clutching a letter in her hand.

"You're still here."

"Well I almost jumped out of my skin but yes, I am still here. What is going on?" Naomi demanded, throwing her legs over the side of the twin bed and rubbing her eyes.

"We thought you had gone with him," Anke answered crisply, also entering the room. She snatched the paper out of Emma's hand and flung it at Naomi.

"Gone with who? Guys, it's a little early in the morning for brain teasers. Can you tell me what is happening or can I go back to bed?"

"Do you know anything about this?"

Naomi picked up the single sheet of paper and read the note scrawled on the blank canvas.

Dear *Daed, Mammi,* Anke and Emma,

You have always done your best for me but I have never felt like I belonged in this community. I think I always knew that I would leave at some point but it wasn't until Naomi came that I knew the world was calling me. I could not stop thinking about the places she told me, the foods she had eaten, the people she met. I could not understand why she would give that all up to live here, in this boring, judgemental place. I have gone to the city. Don't worry about me, please. I am sure I will make my way just fine. I know this comes as a disappointment but I could not bear the thought of spending my life farming. I love you all.

Yours Always,

Evan

P.S. Tell Naomi if she changes her mind to come and find me in Indianapolis.

Slowly, Naomi read and reread the letter until tears began to slip down her cheeks and blot the ink on the paper. Anke grabbed it and swatted the water from the page scowling.

"*Mamm* and *Daed* haven't read it yet, Naomi. Don't ruin it. You've already ruined enough around here." Anke spun on her heel and stormed out the door, leaving Emma behind. The younger sister looked at Naomi's devastated face and gently placed her hand upon her shoulder.

"I told you to stay away from Evan," she murmured. "Not because you're not good enough for him but because he is not good enough for you."

<u>**May**</u>

"Naomi, you have been moping around here for a month now. I miss your sunny smile," Bishop Kurtz told her one day as he passed by the farm.

"I am not moping, Bishop!" Naomi protested. "I am working!"

"Yes, yes you are working and doing a fine job, I might add," he agreed. "But you need to forget about Evan. I understand you were very fond of him."

"He was my friend." Naomi dropped the hoe and stared at the bishop. The look was enough to stop him from uttering his next thoughts but his eyes travelled over her head to look at something in the distance.

"Well, I still miss your smile, child," he told her. "And sometimes when God closes a door, he opens up a window." She followed his gaze as he turned to leave and she saw Camp approaching in a wagon.

"Good day, Naomi," Camp greeted, somewhat nervously. "Would you care to go for a ride? I have an appointment with a medical doctor in town today."

Immediately, Naomi was concerned.

"Are you all right?" she asked, hurrying forward, wiping her dirty hands on her apron.

"Oh yes. Nothing serious. But I wouldn't mind the company," he replied. Naomi nodded quickly. *It is serious enough for him to ask her for companionship after an estrangement*, she thought nervously.

"Just give me a minute to change."

She was beside him in the carriage in minutes and they rode silently for a while.

"Naomi, when are you going to stop brooding about?"

"I am not brooding!" she snapped. *I'm not brooding! I am pining. Evan could come back any day. That is not brooding or moping. That is called being hopeful.*

"Fine." They continued their trip quietly. Naomi realized how unfair she was being to Camp. Camp was there. Evan was not. Camp stood by her. Evan hadn't even asked if she wanted to go with him. Why would she not give Camp a chance?

"I'm sorry, Camp," she finally said. He shot her a look out of the corner of his eye.

"What for?"

"I don't deserve your affections. You have been too good to me since the beginning."

"You are very worthy of all things good, Naomi. It has been my pleasure you call you my friend."

Naomi looked at him, his noble face proud and unsmiling.

"Would it be your pleasure to call me your wife?"

October

When their engagement was announced at worship, Naomi was met with genuine adulation.

"Camp Giron is a fine man. He will be Bishop one day, I promise you. You have made the right decision," Bishop Kurtz told her. "And I do believe you have made the man very happy. I have known Camp since he was a boy. I could count the amount of times he has smiled on one hand since then. Until you came along, Naomi. He adores you."

"He is a wonderful man," Naomi agreed, shooting her fiancé a look from across the salon. He met her gaze and smiled. Bishop Kurtz opened his mouth to say something else but seemed to reconsider.

"I hope you two will be very happy together, Naomi."

"I hope so too," she replied, a sudden stab of sadness overwhelming her. She would be lying to herself to say she didn't still think of Evan. She wondered if he was faring well in the city and if he ever thought about her. She knew that he wasn't coming back.

"He would not be welcome here if he did," Anke spat when Naomi asked her about him one night. Naomi had been shocked at the venom attached to his sister's words. Later, Emma pulled her aside.

"I know you were rather fond of my brother," Emma told her. "But there are many things you did not know about him."

Naomi arched an eyebrow. She wasn't sure she wanted to hear anything negative about Evan but curiosity got the better of her.

"Such as?" But Emma pursed her lips together as if she had already said too much.

"Just believe me, Naomi. You are marrying a good man in Camp. He will always do right by you." The words meant little to Naomi who lay awake at night, listening for sounds, dreaming that Evan would sneak back into the house and into her life again.

<u>November</u>

"You are a lovely bride," Emma whispered, adjusting the wreath of flowers about Naomi's head. Naomi smiled genuinely and gave her a hug.

"I don't think I've ever thanked you for all you've done for me, Emma," she told the younger girl. The blonde blinked and looked confused.

"What have I done?"

"You have helped give me a sense of community and family, one I have never had. I know you don't think I belong here but I want you to know that I care more about these people and our way of life than anyone or anything I have before in my life."

"I know you belong here, Naomi. That is why I asked Bishop Kurtz to speak with you. Camp and I saw the purity in your soul from the first day we met you. You are exactly the kind of person we want walking among us." The women smiled at each other and for the first time since Evan had left, Naomi felt truly happy. *I do belong here. I am one of them. Thanks to Emma and Bishop Kurtz. And thanks to Camp.*

"Shall we?" Emma offered Naomi her arm and the two made their way into the church where Camp stood waiting at the altar. Naomi felt like she was seeing him for the first time. He looked so handsome, his dark hair shining under his hat, two glossy curls hanging about his chiseled features. His eyes were alight with adoration as he watched his bride to be slowly walk toward him. His face broke into a beam so broad, Naomi was sure his face would crack from the force. Tears misted his irises. Emma gently squeezed her arm and released toward Camp. Suddenly, an abrupt gust of wind flew through the small chapel, extinguishing several of the lamps. Bride and groom turned toward the entrance where a form stood, panting in the opened doorway.

"Evan!" Naomi gasped. Immediately, Mr. Hilty rose to his feet, his face crimson in anger.

"How dare you show your face in here!" he thundered.

"I am not here for you, *Daed*," Evan retorted, his eyes remaining on Naomi as he stumbled up the aisle.

"Naomi, don't marry him!" he called as he approached. "Come back to the city with me. I made a mistake leaving you here but you're all I can think about." A murmur flowed through the crowd. *He did think about me! He does miss me!* Naomi thought, dumbfounded. Evan was at the altar, grabbing for her hands, his blue eyes pleading.

"I'm sorry! I made a mistake," he said again, his mouth turning up into a smile of contrition. Naomi glanced up at Camp, who had lost the rare beam which had lit up the church. She looked at Emma who shook her head woefully and stared at her shoed. Her gaze shifted to Bishop Kurtz whose mouth had formed a fine line. She stared into the crowd and took in Evan's family's look of shame and fury. Then she looked back at Camp again.

"I'm sorry," she whispered at him and Camp hung his head in defeat, his shoulders visibly sagging. Evan tightened his grip on her hands and Naomi yanked them back, her eyes still trained on Camp.

"I am sorry," she said again, reaching up to wipe the tears falling onto his cheeks. "I am sorry that I ever made you hurt. I am so sorry that I wasted any time on this man. I am so terribly sorry that I ever doubted my future is in your arms. I love you, Camp." She turned furiously to Evan who had gone pale at Naomi's speech.

"But Naomi – "

"What kind of disgusting man claims to love a woman and leaves her for months only to barge in on her wedding? You're despicable, Evan. And you're not welcome in our community – my community! Get out and don't return." After a stunned second of silence, Evan whirled on his heel and ran out the door.

"And you don't even close the door behind you! Can you imagine marrying such a man?" Naomi yelled after him. Applause and laughter broke out and someone hurried to shut the double doors and relight the kerosene lamps. Naomi took Camp's hands in hers and they gazed into each other's eyes lovingly.

"Now, where were we?" she asked Bishop Kurtz without looking away.

END

AMISH AMITY

Chapter 1

Rain just kept falling, never ending without any intention to stop, large puddles had gathered on the muddy grounds around the big barn, and water gushed down the eroded embankment running alongside the road, causing the road to be completely flooded. But no amount of rain would prevent Amity, Betty and Rachel to do what they came here to do. Having been friends since childhood, the three women were inseparable. Neither of them were married or promised to anyone yet, and although they are well beyond the age most girls in their community starts to settle down to start a family, it never really bothered them.

Amity was strong willed and mouthy young woman, who voiced her opinion whenever she felt it mattered. Of course her father, Bishop Gunther didn't quite approve of her behaviour at times, but he did support her willingness to stand up for herself. Bishop Gunther on the other hand wasn't like most others in their faith; he was more lenient and accepting than most, always promoting change within reason. He insisted that households started using gas stoves instead of coal stoves. He had even arranged to buy a truck to help the community to cart goods to the local market in town. According to him, modern change to a bare minimum does not give the devil a foothold, it just shows the devil that they are capable of change without modern ways ruling their lives and changing who they are or distracting them from things that matter most.

Betty, much like Amity also had a strong personality, one she definitely got from her mother, but she also had a mischievous streak. When the elders instructed the children not to play in the rain, she was always the first to splash in muddy puddles. When they had their social events, she was the one who would pull pranks, like stuff a mouse in someone's pocket or stick a dish to a table cloth with workman's glue, causing a huge disaster when someone tries to pick it up. All innocent pranks at most, but that was how everyone knew her and more often than not, when she was younger her father would ground her for punishment, but she always found a way out of it.

And then there was Rachel, shy quiet Rachel. More like the runt of the litter, she was one of few words and always just tagged along because Amity and Betty insisted. Rachel only had a father; her mother died giving birth to her. Her father eventually married Elsa, a widow with two sons, who she never got on with. They were two brats and she ended up spending more time with her friends than her own family and over the years, the trio had become the best of friends

Betty giggled and Amity squirmed on the bale of hay, "I bet you David looks like that when he takes his shirt off," she said pointing to the male model in the fashion magazine.

Amity giggled, "It's scandalous! If your dad knew you had these, he'll shun us all," she said in jest.

Rachel, curious as ever, was sitting on the left, also peeking at the magazine, one of the few they kept hidden in the barn under one of the wooden floor slats. They always snuck to the barn to page through the magazines and weigh every other man in their town up against the likes of models that posed so shamelessly with nothing but pair of underpants on.

"*Jah!* Well he doesn't know now does he?" Betty said and paged through a few more pages.

Rachel would never admit it out rightly but she also felt a slight tingle of excitement when she looked at these magazines, they were not overly crude, but they showed more flesh than she had ever seen in her life. Maybe it was because of this, that they were all still single, she thought. Comparing the local boys to those men were like comparing apples with onions.

A sudden noise quickly alerted them and Betty shoved the magazine behind the bale of hay they were seated on. Both Amity and Betty grabbed their egg baskets, while Rachel stood around looking as guilty as ever.

"Betty, are you girls here?"

It was Betty's father who called, and Rachel's stomach lurched, if the Bishop had any idea what they were up to they will be in so much trouble.

"We're here *daed*!" Betty called and dusted the hay off of her dress, "We were caught in the rain, and was waiting for it to pass," she said as her Bishop Gunther appeared.

"I thought so, well I have come to get you girls home, the storm is a long way from being over," he said and handed each of them a rain coat, "Better we hurry, or the storm will catch up with us," he urged them as he let each one of the girls walk towards the barn door ahead of him.

The sky was dark and it wasn't just a summer shower, it was a downpour that looked more like a waterfall from heaven. Heavy drops struck the ground tunnelling into the earth. Up ahead stood the buggy, which didn't offer much or any shelter and Rachel wasn't so sure if they would make it to their respective homes in one piece. Betty was the first to step into the rain, followed by Amity. Bishop Gunther looked at her and nodded, and then in a huddled group the four of them ran towards the buggy, careful not to slip and fall.

Thankful that there was still some daylight to guide the way, the three girls clung to each other as Betty's father steered the buggy towards the house. Hardly able to see a few feet ahead of them and on a treacherous road that has been washed away in most places, Bishop Gunther was still able to make them feel at ease. He didn't even look worried, but then again, that was probably how a man of God should be, like Paul walking on water.

The buggy wheels rattled as they rode over rocks and muddy trenches formed by the mass of water running diagonally across the small road. And a trip that normally took less than fifteen minutes to travel, now seemed like an eternity. They were slowly making their way ahead through the stormy downpour, unbeknownst to Bishop Gunther, the road up ahead had turned into complete sludge and the moment the buggy reached it, the wheels simply slid into a deep trench on the side of the road, pulling the buggy, with the horse off and on to the side of the road. The girls screamed in panic as the buggy slowly leaned over to its side, threatening to topple over. Rachel was the first to clobber out and then helped the other two on to the road. Betty got out safely, but as Amity stumbled out of the buggy, she stepped in a hole and twisted her ankle.

"Ow!!" she cried out as she fell to the ground grabbing for her ankle.

"Amity!" Betty cried and ducked down to help her friend, "Where does it hurt?"

Bishop Gunther also hunched down and looked at her ankle, "It's quite swollen, I think you may have sprained it, can you try and step on it?"

Betty and her father helped Amity to her feet, but the moment she put weight on her injury, she cried out in agony.

"We will have to get you home, just lean on me and Betty" the Bishop said. He studied the state of the buggy, "The buggy will have to stay here until morning."

"But papa, we can hardly see in front of us," Betty lamented as she supported her friend.

"The Lord will light our way," Rachel said confidently and gave Betty a gentle reassuring squeeze.

With Amity supported by Bishop Gunther and Betty, and Rachel next to them carrying the egg baskets, they started down the path taking carful steps in the dark.

Through the stormy gale and rain that kept showering, they heard a galloping sound that sounded more like thunder coming towards them and the next moment, a man on horseback arrived completely drenched.

Rachel couldn't make out his face, but right now he was the best thing that could have happened to them.

"Bishop, Maryanne sent me to see what was keeping you," he shouted over the raging storm, "What happened to the buggy?"

Rachel took over from the Bishop, while he explained to the stranger exactly what had happened, and suggested that they come to recover the buggy in the morning once the rain has passed.

"Betty, you will have to get on the horse with Amity, Rachel you will walk with Uri and I," the Bishop instructed and then the stranger named Uri, helped Amity, and then Betty on to the horse.

Together they slowly made their way back to society, the first stop was Amity's house, where the Bishop helped to get her inside, and seen to, then it was Rachel's turn and finally Uri, Bishop Gunther and Betty made their way to the Bishop's house.

~*~

After Rachel had changed into her night dress and towel dried her wet hair, she deposited herself in front of the fire place. The night had turned out a complete disaster. She was sure it was punishment for their bad behaviour. Lusting like that over fictitious men and so on. She wrapped her quilt around her shoulders and reached for her bible. She knew better than to let her judgement be influenced by anyone. Despite the guilt, she somehow found her mind drifting to the stranger who came to their aid. She still couldn't see his face clearly, but she was sure he was handsome, and strong.

She shook her head to chase away the thoughts and closed her eyes, and said a silent prayer of repentance. She was never going to look at those magazines again.

Chapter 2

The sun broke through the parted curtains in Rachel's room and she pinched her eyes shut. The night before had taken its toll on her, and resulted in her oversleeping when there was still so much to do. She was yet to feed the geese and get ready to go to the local market to deliver the eggs she had collected the day before, but she simply had no will power.

"Rachel!" Her step-mother called from the kitchen, "Come have your breakfast!"

Rachel covered her eyes with her forearm and sighed. She just needed a few more minutes of sleep, but she knew where her priorities lay. She willed herself out of bed and rushed around the room to get ready for the day. By the time she got to the kitchen her mother had already cleaned the dishes, and Rachel's breakfast was waiting.

"The Bishop and his friend were here earlier," Elsa commented in passing, "Looks like you girls had a rough night."

"Yeah, we got caught in the storm," she mumbled.

So the stranger is one of the Bishop's friends, which means he was old, she thought to herself.

"Apparently Amity had twisted her ankle quite badly, but she will be fine in a few days."

"I figured. She stepped in a hole when she tried to get out of the buggy, we couldn't see much."

Elsa came to sit at the table with her, "You girls need to be more careful, things could have been a lot worse."

Sometimes Rachel couldn't help but wonder what Elsa's agenda really was. At times she treated her like a stranger, barely paying attention to her, and other times she came across all motherly. And all this time Rachel had no choice but to keep her own emotions all bottled up.

"We will," Rachel said and stood up to wash her plate, "I'm taking the eggs to the market, is there anything you need me to do?"

"Oh not to worry about the eggs, I've already sold delivered them this morning."

Rachel felt as if she could crush the plate in her hands. Those eggs were her eggs, her income. She was saving money for herself, and now Elsa had taken the little bit she could earn for herself.

"Thank you," she said tight lipped without turning around.

"I hope you don't mind, your father does need some money to buy that new gas stove so, I figured every penny would help."

"Of course," Rachel turned around this time, with a fake smile plastered on her face, "I'll just get more eggs to get money for my new dress."

"Why on earth would you need a new dress?" Elsa said with mock surprise, "Don't you have enough as it is?"

Rachel was slowly starting to lose her temper, but she fought hard to remain calm, "I only have three dresses, and I need one for church, the others are all worn and faded."

Elsa laughed, "It's not like you'll be catching anyone's eye, and you're past the point of marriage. You're already considered a spinster."

"I'm only twenty-two, the same age my mother married," Rachel protested.

"And see how that turned out."

Elsa had barely said the words when her sons, Caleb and Alfred came into the kitchen, and Rachel had to hide her anger. She simply scooped up her empty egg baskets and stormed out of the house. How that woman dared say such heartless things and get away with it, was beyond her she thought as she marched determinedly in no particular direction. But as the anger subsided, it was replaced by doubt. Maybe it was too late for her to marry, but then the same applied to Betty and Amity, they were both the same age. Obviously living in Derby Creek wasn't much help either, there were far more women than men here, and unless they had gatherings from nearby towns, chances of finding a suitor was slim.

First of all there was Betty, who insisted that she was waiting for Mr Right, she refused to settle for less, then there's Amity who also had her own ideas of a suitor, and the few men that did ask for her hand in the past, were coldly turned down because she was just not interested. Rachel always thought that Amity was the kind who would go on a Rumspringa if her father allowed her, out of the three friends, she was the adventurous one.

Rachel grunted a loud oomph as she collided with someone sending her baskets flying. Thankfully they were empty; otherwise they would both have been covered in egg yolk. She stumbled back and started to apologize profusely when she swallowed her words, and a pair of very strong hands cupped her shoulders.

"Are you alight?" the young man asked, and offered her a lopsided smile.

"Jah, I am fine, I-I wasn't paying attention, I'm sorry," she said struggling to breathe.

"It's quite alright, you were miles away there for a second, I'm Uri, Rachel right?" he said and released her as he tucked his thumbs into his suspenders.

Uri, the name immediately rang a bell. He was Bishop Gunther's friend, but how? He was so young, she wondered.

"How do you know my name?" she asked foolishly.

"I came to your rescue last night in the storm, but I suppose you won't recognise me, it was rather dark."

"Oh! Oh right, yes. Well... um, I'll be going now. Thank you, I mean sorry, I... I have to go."

Rachel just about ran away from him, she had acted like a complete and utter fool, stuttering over her words like a second grader having to do an oral assignment. No wonder she was single. She couldn't sit in the company of a man without feeling awkward. As she hurried away she could feel his eyes burn into the back of her, but she refused to glance back. The farther she got away the quicker her out of control heart and raging butterflies would quieten down.

"Rachel!" It was Betty who waved her down, "Where are you heading?"

"Eggs!"

"You're going to Eggs?" Betty giggled.

"No, ugh, I'm going to collect eggs silly," she corrected herself as Betty fell into step next to her, "How is Amity doing?"

"She's fine, but you look like you've seen a ghost, why are you in such a hurry," Betty said as she tried to keep up to Rachel's pace.

"I need to sell enough eggs to buy a new dress. The cow sold all the eggs I collected yesterday."

"What a cow, did she not even ask you?"

"Does she ever?"

The rest of the way, the two friends walked in silence, Betty on her own planet, and Rachel trying to get Uri out of her mind. She hadn't expected him to be so young, nor did she expect him to know her name. The night before was a bit of a blur with everything going on, and she mostly remembered walking beside Bishop Gunther while Uri guided the horse by its reins with Amity and Betty on horseback.

"Is Uri your..."

"Don't you think Uri is..."

They both said at the same time and then burst out laughing.

"Uri is so handsome," Betty continued, "The last time I saw him was when we were kids. His family has been in Germany for the past few years."

"I didn't expect him to be so young," Rachel said, "Are they staying here?"

"Only Uri, he's staying at our house and is helping papa with a few things."

Rachel could hear by Betty's tone that she was keen on Uri, and she knew by the seam of her dress, that Amity will be just as taken by him.

One of them will most certainly catch his eyes, she thought and smiled softly. Her friends or at least one of them deserved a good strong man to care for them.

She dismissed the notion of Uri straight away, knowing that she would never stand a chance. She could hardly string together a proper sentence when she bumped into him earlier.

Chapter 3

Amity humped along with a crutch in one hand, while Betty excitedly skipped besides them. For the first time in who knows how long, Betty and Amity had made some effort to look presentable, both of them had brand new dresses. It was the Friday night frolic, where most boys got to voice their intentions.

Betty was nervous; as usual she was shy and nervous. She never liked these events much, she did not trust the thing called love, her father loved once, he had promised his her mother that he would make sure she was taken care of, but now years later, all she had to remember her mother by was a single letter, and a lifetime of regret. Elsa was kind in some ways, but she was jealous of Betty, and Betty never did much right in her eyes.

The people from the surrounding farms started to arrive, old and young, in the middle of the big barn the table was set as always. Food in excess was spread across the table, along with lanterns casting a dim glow over everything.

"Have you seen how handsome Uri is?" Betty whispered under her breath.

Amity giggled and shifted in her chair, "I know right? I can still feel his hands on my hips as he helped me on to the horse."

"Oh and weren't they the biggest stronger hands ever?" Betty swooned.

"I'm going to make a play for him you know?" Amity murmured under her breath.

"No you're not, I am, and I've already spent some quality time with him."

Betty wagged her brows and reached for bunch of grapes.

"You can't eat now, we have to say thanks first," Amity said slapping Betty's hand.

"Oh please, no one is even looking."

Betty listened to her friends as they cooed over the newcomer and she opted not to show any interest. They had reason to try and win his affection, she had none. She will see this night through and make the best of a bad situation. Besides, she had a lot more on her mind. Maybe it was time she accepted the fact that she was a spinster, and she figured it was time she spoke to the Bishop and go his take on her moving out of her paternal home into her own. She could always offer her help as a teacher. She knew how to read, in fact she loved reading. She could go spend time at the local school and read to the youngsters, even help the school teachers to give extra lessons in literacy.

"Rachel!" Amity's voice broke into her thoughts.

"Oh... sorry I wasn't listening," she apologised.

"I was saying, maybe all three of us should play for Uri, we can see which one he picks."

Rachel raised her brows, "He's not up for auction, it's a silly game you're wanting to play."

"Stop being such a drab! It will be fun."

No it won't, she thought. The first thing that is bound to happen is that Uri will pick either Betty or Amity, then that will leave one or the other angry and disappointed, ruining a friendship of many years.

"I'm not a drab, I'm just saying. What if he picks Betty, then you'll be angry, not?"

Amity rolled her eyes, "You take things way to seriously, if he picks Betty, then so be it, I'm hardly desperate to marry."

"Come on Rachel, it will be fun; besides, maybe he shows no interest in any of us, then at least we know we all tried."

Betty worried her lip and looked down at her hands, "I don't know, I suppose no harm can come of it." She for one knew that she won't be the least bit phased if he picked Amity or Betty, because she knew she stood no chance.

Amity shoved her elbow into Rachel's ribs and gestured with her head towards the door. Talk of the devil, Uri was heading straight down the path on the opposite side of the table with his eyes fixed on them. And once again the sight of him made her heart race and as she watched him approach it was as if all else around her faded. She had tunnel vision and it was only him looking straight at her. When he finally stopped and took a seat directly opposite her she averted her eyes immediately. Of course, Amity kicked her under the table and Rachel cleared her throat uncomfortably.

"*Hallo* Uri," she said.

"*Hoe gaan het*, Rachel?" he smiled.

She only nodded, her tongue felt like led in her mouth, and her palms were sweaty.

Betty and Amity both fell right into conversation, putting their best foot forward while Rachel wanted nothing but to flee. Soon enough the evening got on the way, with youngsters all frolicking and enjoying the event. Uri made sure he mingled with everyone and never let on that he was interested in any of them in particular, which was funny, since Betty put her best foot forward and out rightly told him he had beautiful eyes.

As the evening drew to a close and most of the people had left, the last remaining few spent the rest of the time talking about the up and coming barn raising event. Uri was still seated across from Rachel, and Betty and Amity had moved closer to where Bishop Gunther was. He was playing the harmonica, which was probably the only instrument allowed in the community, but still sounded like heaven.

"So Rachel, have you always lived here?" Uri asked curiously as he picked on some of the bread sticks on his plate.

"*Jah*, I was born here," she said and offered him a shy smile.

"I'm surprised I don't remember you?"

"I'm not exactly the most memorable of all," she laughed.

"Oh but you are, you are a very beautiful woman."

Rachel blushed profusely and covered the side of her face with her hand, "Thank you," she mumbled.

"Can I pick you up for church on Sunday?"

Shocked at his request, Rachel shifted uncomfortably in her seat and worried her lip, as tempting as it was, she wasn't so sure if it was a good idea. But then again, Betty and Amity did say that they should all try and win his affection. She looked down at her empty plate and smiled. Perhaps it was time she stepped out of her comfort zone and tried dating at least, after all, he was simply going to take her to church, and it wasn't like he was proposing to her at all.

"Sure," she said and then got up, "I have to go now. I will see you around."

She saw his mouth open and close, but she rushed away regardless. She said her goodbyes to her friends and the rest of the community who were all still in the barn and headed home. Her mind was racing and her heart even more. For the life of her she couldn't understand what Uri saw in her. *You're a beautiful woman* – he had said, and it made her feel as if she was about to fly into the night sky on wings of angels. No boy, or man for that matter, had ever paid her such a compliment, and coming from someone as handsome and Uri, made her tummy do strange things.

Chapter 4

Uri was up and ready long before dawn on Sunday, making sure his buggy was clean and that he too was dressed in his best church clothes. He couldn't deny the fact that he felt bad for Betty, she had shown her affection so openly, but there was just no chemistry between them. Unlike Rachel, Betty was just too flamboyant to his liking. She was a pretty woman, but not even nearly as pretty as Rachel. Rachel was unusually pretty, with red hair that always seemed so perfectly plated and rolled up under her prayer cap, with loose strands that tickled her cheeks. The slight dusting of freckles across her nose, that spread to her cheeks made her even prettier, almost innocent not to mention the way she blushed every time he spoke to her.

He was quite surprised when she accepted his request to start off with, but pleased nonetheless.

The first night he saw the shy girl, with her baskets filled with eggs, he was intrigued. She was in control despite the stormy weather and their predicament, and even when he lifted the other two on to the horse, she never uttered as single complaint. She walked quietly next to them as if she was taking a stroll. Not even the rain slanting heavily against them broke through her composure. Maybe it was the way she kept to herself, or the way her eyes lit up the next day when he bumped into her, he wasn't quite sure himself, but if he had to pin it to one thing, it was God's will. It was God's will that he returned to Derby Creek after all these years and God had sent the storm so that he could meet his future wife.

"Uri, you're up early," Betty said as she entered the kitchen where he was having his morning tea.

"Jah, up and ready for church," he said and grinned excitedly.

She came to sit next to him and perched her chin on her hand, looking at him all dreamy eyed. Shifting slightly to get some distance, he smiled and shoved the plate of rusks closer to her.

"I'm on my way to collect Rachel for church," he announced, not sure how Betty would react.

From day one, she had made it no secret that she fancied him; neither did Amity, so it was better if he got it out in the open before either of them got their hopes up.

"Rachel?" Betty said scrunching up her face, "Have you asked her then?"

He nodded and took the last sip of his tea, "Jah, she's a shy one, but she accepted my offer."

Betty scratched her head and slumped back in her chair, and Uri could just imagine what thoughts were flitting through her mind, hoping that this would not ruin their friendship. But when Betty stood up and held her hand up for a high-five, he grinned.

"She's a dear friend, but a nervous wreck, you best make sure you treat her right," Betty grinned, "She's had a lot of hardship with that stepmother of hers."

Uri frowned, tempted to ask about this stepmother, but held back. If anyone was going to tell him about Rachel, it was Rachel herself. He would want for no secrets or tall tales to come from anyone other than her.

He looked at the clock against the wall in the kitchen and took his hat, nodded at Betty and headed out. For a man nearing his thirties, he felt like teenager himself.

~*~

Rachel waited outside for Uri's arrival and her stomach was doing wild flips, while her heart was missing beats every so often trying to keep up the pace. She had never entertained the advances of a man, and had no idea how to behave in the presence of one who had made his intensions clear. A boy simply did not offer a girl a ride in his buggy unless he was interested in her as more than a friend. This was serious business. She also omitted to let her father know, because she knew that Elsa would have a hundred and one things to say about it. She shifted on the swing chair changing her position, trying to find the one that made her feel most at ease, but her body felt awkward. Her arms felt as if they were too long, her legs felt numb and overall her body and mind appeared to be disconnected. Tired of trying to figure out the best seating position she stood up and paced up and down the porch, and then finally she opted for leaning against the pillar. Just in time too, as she heard the nearing rumble of a buggy, which could only have been Uri.

When he came to a stop in front of her gate, she quickly rushed down the stairs.

"Morning Rachel, you look lovely today," Uri said as he climbed out and came around to help her in.

"Good morning," she said softly.

"Did you sleep well?"

"Jah, I did, thank you."

It took her some time to loosen up and say more than four words at a time, but Uri had this amazing ability to make her feel free. With him she didn't have to count every word, or watch her tongue. She could just say what she wanted. On their way to church, he asked her about the things she likes most. The talked about her life, and her family, she didn't feel like she needed to hide anything from him at all. She even admitted how she felt about Elsa, which made her feel less restricted. At church, they didn't sit next to each other, but Betty and Amity were curious as ever.

"So he picked you did he?" Amity whispered under her breath.

"I don't know, maybe," Rachel murmured.

"You're blind as a bat; everyone can see he likes you."

Rachel blushed and kept her head down, her friends were impossible and as much as she tried to pay attention to the service she couldn't. If it wasn't for Betty or Amity, whispering to her under their breaths, it was the sure awareness of Uri watching her. And that did not go unnoticed by her friends either.

By the time the service had come to an end, Rachel couldn't wait to get outside to catch a breath of fresh air, and steal a moment for herself, but it was short lived.

"You never told us you're meeting a boy?" Elsa said as she came to stand next to Rachel.

"I didn't know I needed your permission," Rachel said blankly.

"Well I suppose you are old enough to make your own, but you know, Albert will be very disappointed that you never told him."

Rachel knew exactly what Elsa was playing at, and this time she was not going to let the woman who pretends to care throw any hurdles in her way.

"I think he'll live, and you should be too pleased that I won't be a bother to you for much longer."

Talk about rushing into things, Rachel thought as she hurried away from Elsa, it wasn't as if Uri was going to ask for her hand in marriage, they hardly knew each other. But even if that wasn't the case, whatever happened, come the beginning of winter, she would move out anyway and start her own life, with or without a husband.

Chapter 5

Uri had spent most of the time getting to know Rachel, and the more he got to know her, the more he was convinced that she was the perfect wife for him. He had spent almost every evening visiting with Rachel and in the past few months since they started their courtship he got to know a woman, who despite her adversities in life, rose above it all. Her stepmother no longer tried to boss her around, and her father was too pleased that his only daughter is finally blooming.

It was a perfect autumn day; the ground was covered in a carpet of reds and golds that reminded him of Rachel. He had already asked her father for her hand in marriage, and although it didn't quite follow the custom of dating for an extended period, he saw no reason to wait. They were both adults who were in love and certain of one thing, their own happiness.

As usual he waited patiently for Rachel to exit the house, and like two curious toddlers Amity and Betty was not far away either. They had both come to terms with the fact that he had made his choice, and they were extra supportive of Rachel too. As he whispered a silent prayer for guidance, Rachel made her appearance as if the Lord had answered his prayer. Today was the day he was going to ask her for her hand in person.

"Good morning Uri," she said and her smile lit up his world.

"Morning to you Rachel, you look absolutely radiant today," he complemented her and it earned him an even wider smile.

"I made myself a new dress, do you like it?"

"It's beautiful," he said and held out his hand.

He could already imagine the gasps and giggles coming from the two friends as he struggled to find the right words. He had rehearsed it so well, but now here in the moment, he was at a loss for words.

"Are you alright?" she asked and placed the back of her hand against his cheek, "You look flustered."

Uri cleared his throat and caught her hand, keeping it against his cheek, "I'm fine, but there is something I would like to ask you."

Rachel tilted her head and her hazel eyes sparkled with curiosity as she waited for him to speak.

"Go on!" Betty shouted from across the road!

Uri closed his eyes and smiled, they weren't helping him at all.

"Uri?" Rachel said softly, "What is it?"

He took a deep breath, and then took both her hands in his, "Rachel, I have spoken to your father, and I would be honoured if you would agree to become my wife."

The way Rachel's expression changed from being concerned to completely surprise was priceless. She didn't have to answer him at all, because the way her lips tugged into a wide smile and her eyes filled with tears, he knew she wouldn't turn him down.

Rachel flung her arms around his neck and buried her face in the crook of his neck and whispered, "I thought you'd never ask."

Uri chuckled, "I was hoping you would accept."

"Why would I not?" she said and smiled lovingly up at him.

A FORK IN THE AMISH ROAD

ABIGAIL DUNCAN

Chapter One

Emily kicked her feet along the dirt path, struggling with her heavy suitcase beneath the late-August sun. Everything looked exactly the same as she remembered it from the last time she'd been there, nearly seven years ago to the day.

She'd never expected to be back there.

There were people staring at her from the houses that she passed along the road. She could feel their eyes on her as she trudged past. But she didn't look to see who was watching her. She didn't need them to think she was worried.

They must already know exactly how she felt anyway.

When she reached her parents' house, she kicked open the gate and slowly walked up the front path, then stood hesitantly on the faded gray porch. After a long moment of composing herself—at least, doing as much as she could to compose herself, which admittedly wasn't much beyond taking a few deep breaths and smoothing her hands along her dress—she raised her hand to knock firmly on the door.

Her mother answered. She didn't say a single word —and she definitely didn't move to embrace her daughter, although she hadn't seen Emily in nearly seven years now. Instead, she just stared long and hard at the woman. "Don't let your father see you before you've seen the minister," she said finally, closing the door in Emily's face.

Emily sighed and released her grip on her suitcase, falling into a heap there on the front porch with tears stinging her eyes.

After a long moment of hopelessness, though, she dragged herself up off the ground. She gave one last despairing look at her suitcase before shoving it off to the side, resolving to leave it there until she returned. Because she would be returning, she vowed. No matter what the minister said, she wasn't going to allow it to drive her out of the community. Not again.

She took a deep, shaky breath and scrubbed her hands along the coarse fabric of her dress one last time.

The minister's porch was shaded by a large oak tree in the yard, and the cool air was a welcome reprieve from the stuffy heat, but there was nothing that could cure the racing of her heart at this point. In a community like this, what the minister said could make or break a person. If she managed to curry the minister's favor, it was smooth sailing from there on out. But after her indiscretions and stupid, rebellious teenage years, she'd be lucky if the man would even talk to her.

With her daughter sleeping somewhere in New York City, in her ex-husband's house, she'd be lucky if the man would even look at her.

In her youth, there had been one other man who was shunned by the community. David had been a good man, as far as she'd known, but he and his father hadn't seen eye-to-eye on something—to this day, no one really knew what, although the rumors were all over the board. She'd never understood why someone would choose to go against their whole community for a gamble at the outside world. It wasn't like the outside world really held anything that she wanted anyway—it was just vice and unhappiness, as far as she was aware.

Except...

Except there had been Adam. Adam had understood her in a way that no one had ever seemed to understand her before. Adam had made her feel like she was beautiful. Adam had made her feel like...

But it was forbidden to marry outside their Amish community. She'd known that before anything had even started. They'd run around in secret for a while, meeting up in the mountains. She hadn't stopped him when he'd wanted to have sex with her. And it had felt amazing.

Three months later, Emily had been forced to confront the fact that she was pregnant.

That alone was enough to get her expelled from the community. If she'd married Adam, it would have been frowned upon. But getting pregnant outside of a marriage was infinitely worse. Adam had been good to her, though. He'd taken her in and given her and their daughter

Kayla a home, and a year later, the two of them had been married in a small church ceremony in front of Adam's family.

But they'd drifted apart in the years since then. Emily had never really managed to get her feet in the outside world. They'd fought about Kayla's upbringing. Eventually, Adam had asked for a divorce, and she hadn't been able to argue a single reason that they should stay together. Because Adam had a stable job and a stable life, the judge had awarded full custody to him. Emily could still see Kayla if she wanted to, but to be honest, seeing her daughter only brought home to her all the things she'd lost.

She'd returned home without even really planning to. By now, it was a familiar bus route from New York City. It had been a few years since she'd been back with a stack of photographs for James to pass on to her mother, but everything still looked the same. Everything always looked the same. It made the intervening years hurt worse.

The minister answered the door despite the feebleness of her knock. He frowned at her through his glasses. "You shouldn't be here," he said brusquely.

Emily swallowed hard. "I know," she whispered. "But Minister—please. Is there any way I can...repent?" She'd imagined this confrontation so many times, had come up with so many logical reasons to try to persuade him to allow her back into the community. But now she was faced with this moment, all logic had flown from her mind. She broke down into tears. "Please, I just want to come home."

The minister looked at her for a long moment. "That's not possible," he said.

Emily looked pained for a long moment. Finally, one of her arguments drifted back into her head. "I was never baptized," she said. She took a deep breath. "The whole reason that we are baptized is to pledge our commitment to the church and to cleanse us of sin, isn't it? Can't you please..." She trailed off, swiping at a few stray tears. "I'm not asking for things to return to the way they were," she said, her voice barely audible. "I know that that's impossible. But I want to find myself again in this community. I want to dedicate my life to God and do the work that He would have me do. Please."

The minister was silent for a long moment. "I will need to consult with the rest of the community and with God," he said.

Emily bit her lower lip. "I have nowhere to stay until you've decided," she whispered, feeling utterly ashamed at how low she'd fallen. "I left my suitcase on the front porch of my parents' house, but my mother wouldn't even let me inside until I'd spoken to you."

The minister looked thoughtful at that, though. He stood back abruptly. "You look exhausted." He led her into a small room at the back of the house. "It's not much, but it's got a bed. Maybe you'll remember your ties to God by staying here until we've resolved these matters."

Emily could have wept with relief. On a sudden impulse, she reached out and clasped the minister's hand in hers. "Thank you," she told him fervently. She turned her head away as a fresh set of tears began to fall down her cheeks. "It's been so long since I knew such kindness. I've been so lost..."

The minister watched her for a long moment. "As Moses said to Joshua, 'The Lord himself goes before you and will be with you; he will never leave you nor forsake you. Do not be afraid; do not be discouraged.'" He smiled a little at Emily. "I suppose the situation they were speaking about was much direr, but it seems appropriate in this case as well. You have been lost, that's true, but God has never left your side. Turn to him for comfort and you will find that our Lord is a most forgiving God."

Emily took a deep breath and then nodded, brushing the tears from her cheeks. "I can only hope that the community is likewise forgiving," she said grimly.

Chapter Two

The next morning, Emily went out into the minister's garden and prayed for longer than she had in years. By the end of it, she didn't even know what she was praying for anymore—she had passed the point of asking for forgiveness, passed the point of promising all the changes that she wanted to make in her life if he would just let her come back home, and finally reached the point where she was basically meditating there, listening to the silence inside her mind.

It was in this state that James found her.

She could feel his eyes on her as she sat there, but he didn't say anything until she turned her head to look at him. When she saw who it was, she flinched and turned her head away.

James slowly came to kneel down behind her. "Didn't expect to see you here," he said in his gruff voice.

Emily sighed and dropped her head. "Didn't want to tell you everything was falling apart," she said quietly. She bit her lower lip. Admitting all of this to James made everything suddenly seem so real, in ways she wasn't fully ready to deal with. "Adam asked for a divorce. And he got sole custody of Kayla. I mean, it was amicable enough; I'm sure I could still see her, but–"

"But you came running home with your tail between your legs."

Emily felt a surprising bubble of anger inside of her. James had always been on her side before, but now he was acting like... "It's not like it's been easy for me, James," she snapped. "It wasn't easy for me seven years ago when I left, and it isn't easy for me to come back today. Do you know my own mother wouldn't even speak to me until I'd spoken to the minister? And I've lost my husband and I've lost my child, and my life is an utter disgrace, and I–" She broke off and abruptly turned away from him, looking back towards the trees. Any sense of peace she'd found through her meditation was gone now. She took a deep, shaky breath.

"I didn't think it had been easy," James said quietly. "I'm just not sure what you're hoping to find here."

Emily squeezed her eyes shut and pressed her fingertips against the lids. "I don't know," she admitted rawly. "Maybe some sort of a home? Some sense of peace. I feel as though my life has been consumed with chaos since I left here, and I just want..." She trailed off, and then admitted even more quietly, "I've missed you, James. You and I used to be inseparable."

James was silent for a long moment. "I've missed you too," he finally told her. "But Emily, you coming back here isn't going to fix anything. You made your decision a long time ago. You chose Adam and Kayla and the outside world. You can't come back here."

"That's for the minister and the community to decide," Emily said. She rubbed at her wrist. "You make it sound like you don't want me to come back, though."

James sighed. "Maybe I don't. Emily, you complicate things in my life; you know that. Everyone knows that you're the reason I never married."

Emily twisted her fingers together. She didn't know how to respond to that. Fortunately, she was saved having to respond by the arrival of the minister. He stared at the two of them for a long moment, an unreadable look on his face.

Emily stood slowly, taking a couple steps towards the minister with a hopeful look on her face. But the minister shook his head. "The community doesn't trust you to return," he told her flatly. "They believe that given everything you've done, you would corrupt the youth. You don't set the best example for a life with God."

Emily sank back down onto the hard ground, staring emotionlessly at the man.

"That's not fair," James argued, unexpectedly coming to her defense. "Minister, everyone already knows what Emily did. And it's in some ways similar to what a teen experiences during rumspringa, is it not? No one believes that what Emily did was right in abandoning the church and her family, but that doesn't mean she can't atone for her sins or commit herself to the church from now on."

"And what about her husband and her daughter?" the minister challenged. "Will they be joining the church as well? We do not recognize a marriage that is performed outside of our church, and any children born from such a relationship are considered–"

"I'm not married anymore," Emily interrupted. She scrubbed a hand over her face. "Adam left me. Kayla is staying with him. They are no longer part of my life."

James reached over and lightly squeezed her hand. "It'll be all right," he told her. The touch was familiar and comforting, especially given that since she had been shunned, members of the community weren't supposed to show her such affection.

"You don't even want me to be here," Emily retorted, unable to even look at him.

James sighed and shook his head. "It's a little more complicated than that," he admitted.

Emily glanced sadly towards the minister and then slowly pushed herself to her feet. "It's a shame that I'll never get the chance to hear about it," she said quietly. She bowed her head in the direction of the minister. "But of course, if it's the will of the community that I not be allowed to return, then I have no choice but to leave again."

"Where are you going to go?" James asked.

Emily bit her lower lip, tears pricking her eyes. "I don't know," she admitted.

"You only came back because you had nowhere else to go?" the minister asked. "And yet we're supposed to believe you've returned because you want to commit yourself to God and a holy life."

Emily frowned at him. "That's not what this is about at all," she told him. She took a deep breath. "If I wanted to, I could have a well-paying job out in the real world—anywhere I wanted. I have references. I have a resumé. I have skills. I've been working as a secretary, and I could–" She stopped herself, taking a deep breath. "But that's not what I want, don't you see? I wanted a family. I wanted to feel safe and beautiful and happy. And that's why I went off with Adam and why I tried my best to raise Kayla right. But none of that fulfilled me. None of that fed my soul. I need–" She broke off, shaking her head.

"I need to go," she said quickly. "I've already said too much—wasted too much of your time. I need to go." She visibly worked to compose herself, taking a few deep breaths and smoothing her hands over her dress.

"You need to talk to the congregation," James said, glancing over at the minister. "Tomorrow morning, during church. Let them all hear your side of the story before they condemn you to a life of excommunication. Let them hear what it means to you, to be able to come back."

Emily blinked over at him. "They'd never let me–" She looked over at the minister. "Would I be allowed to address them?" she asked him, trying and failing to keep the hopeful note from her voice. "I wouldn't take much of their time, just... I just would want them to know..." She took a shaky breath. "I know that that probably isn't allowed. I shouldn't ask."

The minister was silent for a long moment. "As it happens, my sermon for tomorrow is about forgiveness." He smiled strangely at her. "It's a sermon that I've been working on for weeks now. But I think we could interrupt it in the middle to have a few words from you. And I do think that would be the fair thing to do." He frowned. "Until then, I do have to ask that you not associate with everyone around town. But I'll have a meal on the table at six tonight, if you need something to eat."

With that, the man turned and headed back inside his house.

Emily turned to look at James, feeling utterly incredulous at what she'd just heard. She couldn't stop herself from flinging her arms around the man, even though she knew that that wasn't proper. Even if she weren't currently being shunned by the church, that much public affection was frowned upon. She ought to show restraint. She would need to be better about things like that if she hoped for them to let her come back.

James brought his arms around her as well for a moment, though, pulling her body tight against his. "I've really missed you, Emilyy," he said quietly into her hair. Then he released her and turned away, quickly walking out of the minister's yard.

Chapter Three

The next morning, it seemed like everyone in town was gathered there in the minister's yard. Of course, their church tended to have pretty good attendance, to begin with, but it seemed like there were always people who were too sick to come, or who were needed out in the fields now around harvest time, or who were too old and feeble to make the trek all the way to the minister's house and whom he would go to visit later in the day instead.

She recognized most of their faces still. The ones she didn't recognize, she couldn't spend her time wondering about. Maybe other people had convinced their lovers to join the church and be officially married to them. That was something she'd never been able to convince Adam to do, and seeing so many new faces only made that sting just a little worse. She hoped they would feel some measure of sympathy on her behalf, though.

She took a seat near the back, trying her best to ignore all the curious—and some openly hostile—faces turned towards her. When the minister started speaking, they all turned to face the front of the congregation, and she finally managed to breathe again.

Midway through his sermon, the pastor stopped himself and beckoned for her to come forwards, just as he'd told her he'd do.

Emily rose slowly, keeping her eyes trained on the ground as she moved towards the front. She tried not to focus on the whispers around her, sure that no one was saying anything that she wanted to hear. Finally, after what seemed like an eternity, she turned to face the congregation.

Her eyes searched the crowd, locating first her parents' faces, then her former friends' faces, then—at last—James' face. James was the one who had been with her through all the years, who had helped her smuggle in pictures of Kayla for her mother to see, who had once given her a letter that her mother had written detailing how confused the woman was over Emily's refusal to join the church. James was the one who had always loved her, despite how badly she'd erred over the years.

This confessional was mostly directed towards him.

"I have no right to beg your forgiveness," Emily began, her voice meek but ringing out over the silent congregation. "I have done so many things that I'm not proud of over the last eight years. I have forsaken my family, my friends, and everyone else that I have ever depended on. I went against the church and against our community, and I am not proud of my actions."

She took a deep breath, her eyes scanning the crowd again. "There are a lot of people here that I know I've hurt with my actions—either directly or indirectly." Again, her eyes settled on James. "There are people here who loved me and whom I scorned in return.

"Now I come here, not asking your forgiveness—because the forgiveness that I really need is God's, and I will face that when I reach the gates of Heaven. What I ask you, though, is that you allow me to remain here for the rest of my mortal life, that you allow me back into your community and that you allow me to dedicate the rest of my life towards worshiping God.

"I could have a life in the outside world if I wanted to. I could have a well-paying job in a city skyscraper. But all the money in the world could never fill the void in my soul." She took another deep breath.

"What I truly need, if you're willing to allow it, is a place to come home to, finally. I will spend the rest of my life atoning for the sins that I have committed, and I am happy to do that. But I would like to be baptized, to join this church as a true member of the congregation for the first time in my life, knowing fully well what I've given up and what I'm devoting myself to.

"I'm sure there are people out there right now who don't believe a word that I'm saying, or who think that I'll be a bad influence on your children, or that–" Emily broke off, fighting back a sob. She took a couple deep breaths, trying to compose herself. "I can only hope that there are those of you out there who are willing to give me a second chance to prove who I really am—not the stupid mid-twenties woman who chose to throw away everything she'd ever known, but the early-thirties woman desperate to prove herself to a loving God."

There was silence in the congregation. Emily stood there for a long moment, waiting for some kind of sign—anything to release her from this awkward position. Finally, the minister cleared his throat. "In a true showing of forgiveness, based on everything I've heard and on everything I know of our Lord God, I would officially like to welcome Emily Morgan back into our congregation," he said. "She will be baptized and will make her vows to show her commitment to God."

There was a long silence in the church, until James started clapping. When the rest of the congregation joined in—some of them a bit begrudgingly, albeit, Emily started crying and slipped back to her seat in the back of the room. The rest of the sermon passed like a blur.

Chapter Four

She was hanging out the laundry at her parents' place a week later when James came by. She looked shyly up at him, continuing what she was doing. "How have you been, anyway?" she asked, before he could say anything.

James paused, staring at her, and then shrugged. "Things have been good at the farm," he finally said. "My father taught me well. And over this summer, we finally got the roof up on the new barn and got the building all painted and everything. So things have been pretty good. We're looking at a decent harvest this year, if all goes well."

"That's good," Emily said sincerely. "I'm glad to hear that. If anyone deserves it, it's you."

James snorted. "I wouldn't go that far." He shook his head. "I'm not a saint either, Emily. I didn't do what you did, maybe, but there's no denying that I haven't always seen eye-to-eye with the church either."

Emily paused and then shook out another sheet, keeping her eyes carefully away from his. "I don't know anything about that," she said, clipping the sheet to the line with more force than was strictly necessary. "For all I know, you're a saint." She took a deep breath. "You haven't really told me anything about yourself over the past seven years, James. In all your letters, it's just been...the farm's doing great. And there are stray cats who come around your place looking for milk. And you have a new calf. There's been nothing real, nothing I could..."

"It hurt too much," James said. "Gosh, Emily. Don't you realize how it felt for me to be here by myself, knowing that you were out there with your husband and your daughter? Knowing that I had never been enough for you, that I was never going to be enough for you. Knowing that–"

"I wouldn't go that far," Emily interrupted. She stared down at her hands. "I didn't realize it at the time, of course. You have a different way of telling me how beautiful you think I am. I didn't realize that at the time. I thought because you never vocalized it... I didn't realize that you cared, honestly."

"Because I didn't have sex with you and get you pregnant," James said bitterly.

Emily sighed. "Actually, yes, I guess so. James, I was in my twenties. Everyone wanted to see me married off to someone. Everyone wanted me to fulfill my duty to the church and to God. I'd known you for my entire life, and you..." She shook her head. "I realize it now, I realize that you've always been there for me, regardless of all the stupid things I've done over the years. I know I've probably messed up all the chances I ever had to be with you, now that I've been excommunicated and then somehow exonerated. But I–"

She cut off abruptly as James grabbed her arms and pulled her into a tight hug. The hug was better than any display of affection that she'd ever experienced with Adam, and she practically melted into it.

"I've missed you," she whispered against his plaid flannel shirt. She tightened her grip on him. "You don't even know how much I've missed you."

James sighed and pulled her minutely closer. "I've missed you too," he reminded her. "I'm sure I understand how much you've missed me." He paused. "I still keep wanting to pinch myself. I'm not sure I really believe that you're here."

"What happens now?" Emily asked, pulling away. Her eyes darted from his shoes to the grass to his face and back to his shoes. "You can't... We can't do anything. It would ruin your reputation, and–"

"I don't care about that," James interrupted. "I'm taking you to dinner tomorrow night. I'll see you at seven." He smiled crookedly at her when she finally managed to look up at him. "What, didn't you expect that I would want to take you out, now that you're back?"

"You shouldn't," Emily said, hugging her arms around herself. "You know that's just going to give everyone a reason to shun you as well."

"I'm not doing anything outside of the church," James countered. "I can associate with you without that being reason for anyone to shun me." He shook his head. "We're friends. Everyone has always known that we were friends. And there's nothing weird about me taking you out to dinner as friends."

"Is that what it is?" Emily asked, her eyes narrowing a little. "Are you taking me out to dinner as friends?"

There was a long silence. James finally shook his head. "Emily, you know how I feel about you—I don't think I need to reiterate that. But there's no pressure here. If you want me to be taking you out to dinner as friends, then that's what I'm doing. Or if you're willing to let me take you out to dinner as my oldest friend, as the one girl that I've ever managed to have feelings for—as the one girl I've ever managed to envision having a future with?—then that's what we're doing. But there's no pressure here."

Emily shook her head. "You can't envision having a future with me," she said sadly. "I have Kayla and I have this thing with my past. They've only just let me come back home. Half the time, people won't even talk to me down at the shops."

"That doesn't mean anything," James maintained. "Emilyy, give it time for people to get used to you again. But when it comes to your past, that doesn't bother me, don't you realize that?"

"I'm not asking if it bothers you," Emily protested. "I'm saying that you shouldn't get mixed up with someone like me."

"Someone like you," James echoed. He scrubbed a hand over his face, looking suddenly tired. "What does that even mean? 'Someone like you'—Emily, I've been half in love with you since the third grade, remember? I hate to say it, but there's a reason I've been there for you all these years since you've been together with Adam, and it wasn't just that I had nothing else to do but write letters to you."

Emily shook her head. "You can't—I mean..." She trailed off as James put a finger to her lips.

"I'm taking you to dinner tomorrow night," James persisted. "You can tell yourself whatever you'd like about it. If you want to convince yourself that we're going to dinner as friends, then convince yourself of that If you want to listen to the truth of things and realize that I do actually still want you to be mine, then you can do that instead. But whatever you want to think about it, I'm going to be picking you up around seven, and we're going to walk back to my farm so I can show you what a good cook I've become over the years. And I'm not taking 'no' as an answer this time." He shook his head. "Sometimes I wonder what would have happened if I had got the guts to ask you to dinner nine years ago. But then we wouldn't be the same people now as we've become, would we have?"

Emily shook her head, still feeling amazed at the whole thing. "Okay," she finally said. "Okay. I'll see you tomorrow."

James nodded at her and then turned and strode out of the yard as nonchalantly as though they'd been talking about the weather. Emily stared at him, a bemused look on her face, and then went back to pinning up the laundry.

Chapter Five

The following night, Emily looked in the mirror and nervously smoothed her hands over her dress, trying to decide if this was what she really wanted to wear for her first date with James. The dark gray complemented her eyes well, she knew, but she couldn't help thinking back to when she'd made this dress, ten years ago now. It was actually the dress that she'd always thought she would wear out for her first night with James. But that night had never come.

Until now.

She smoothed her hands over the dress one last time and then turned and walked down to the front door. She wanted to be on the porch by the time James arrived—she didn't especially want her parents to know that James was picking her up on a date.

When James came up to the porch, he was dressed in his nicest suit and suspenders, but his hands were shoved deep in his pockets, as though he were still a nervous teenager come to pick her up.

Emily smiled a little, shaking her head. "Look at you, all dressed up and classy," she said.

James snorted. "Dressed up, maybe. Not quite so classy, unless that's how you want to see me." He held out his arm. "Come on, Emily." He led her slowly down off the porch and then up the dusty road to his place.

Emily wanted to say something, but everything she tried to say fell dead on her lips. "I really have missed you," she finally said into the darkness of the night.

James sighed and tugged her a bit closer, closing his hand over hers. "I've missed you too," he told her. "I didn't know if you would ever be coming back. And I didn't want to hope for you to do so. I know you had your husband and Kayla and that everything in your life was what it was. I wasn't selfish enough to hope that–"

"I've missed you," Emily interrupted. "I had my husband and my daughter and everything else, and I still wanted to come back for you." She stopped moving, pulling James around to face her. "Jamie, you don't know what it's felt like, all these years. To know that I had everything I wanted right there in front of me for so long, and instead, I just..." She shook her head. "I didn't do things the way I was meant to, I suppose. I allowed temptation to lead me astray."

"But you came back," James said, placing his hands on her hips.

Emily gave a fluttering sigh and leaned into him slightly. "I came back," she agreed. She leaned forward, resting her forehead against his collarbone for a moment. "I came back. But you have no idea how ruined I am when it comes to..." She trailed off.

"When it comes to...?" James prompted.

Emily took a deep breath. "James, I've always loved you," she finally managed to say. "From before Adam, from..." She shook her head. "I don't know if I've loved you for as long or as deeply as you've loved me, but I've always loved you. And I'm sorry, okay? I'm sorry that I made this thing with Adam into...such a thing. You deserved better. I deserved better. I just..." She trailed off.

"Shh," James said, bringing his hand up to lightly stroke down her back. "Emily, we were foolish children back then. I couldn't get up the nerve to tell you how I felt, and you couldn't get up the nerve to realize that your storybook romance could be found in someone here in the community—or something." He tilted her head back gently. "I really want to kiss you right now," he admitted. "But that's a luxury that I'm not allowing myself yet."

Emily grinned crookedly at him. "Because you're afraid of where it might lead?"

"No," James said seriously. "Because if we're going to do this, we're going to do this right." He took a deep breath. "Emily Morgan, if you'll let me, I'd like to take you back to my place. I've made a decent meal for the two of us, and when you're ready, I'd like to marry you."

Emily was silent for a long moment, staring up at him there in the twilight. Then, she exhaled a long, shaky breath. "You don't know how much I've wanted that over the years," she finally said, burrowing into his arms. "James, marry me. Make an honest woman out of me for once in my life." She bit her lower lip. "I want to keep you—to protect you, to make you happy, to help you settle into this mortal existence in whatever way I can, to..."

"Emily," James said urgently, bringing his hand up to cup her cheek in his palm. "Emily, you've already helped me with all of that." He smiled crookedly at her. "Remember what I said? Do you want to know why everyone in town thinks you're the reason I never got married? It's because everyone knew, all this time, that I only had eyes for you. It's because everyone knew, all this time, that you were there to make me happy, to help me 'settle into this mortal existence', or whatever else you want to call it. Because you were always, only, the person that I had eyes for."

Emily shook her head, but James drew her eyes back to him with a palm at her cheek. "Emily, I love you more than words could tell," he murmured. "So come have dinner with me. We'll sort out the rest in due time."

Emily could do nothing more than quietly nod.